Dear Kelly:
Thanks! Hope you
enjoy it!
C.I. Dollman
April 2014

A Punk Rock Love Song

By C.I. DeMann

A Punk Rock Love Song

by

C.I. DeMann

Chapter 1

First period lets out and I'm walking to my locker. The hallway's noisy and packed, just like always. People are bumping into me. My bra strap's kind of twisted up, so I'm trying to fix that while I walk, trying to be all casual about it, probably failing. So that's what I'm doing when I see the sign thumbtacked to the wall.

Musicians Wanted.

Piano player seeks guitarist, bassist, and

drummer to play at the

North Sycamore High Follies.

Contact David Nelson if you would like to try out.

I know this will sound weird, but almost as soon as I see this poster, it just seems... important. It feels like it was put there for *me*.

Ridiculous, right? But that's how I feel, standing here in this crowded hallway, looking at this little homemade sign.

See, here's the thing... my mom played bass. And we've still got it. The bass, I mean. And, sure, I don't *really* know how to play it, but still... I've got it. And I used to watch her play it. She always looked so cool. So rockin'. So much cooler than anyone else's mom.

And then, God help me, my eyes start to fill up with tears, right there in the hallway. It's humiliating and I wipe them and probably nobody's even noticed, but still... crying over some stupid sign? Awful. I thought I was past this. It's been six months, for Christ's sake.

Just then, my friend Becky shows up. I don't think she saw me crying.

"Ohmigod, Maggie. Have you seen what Vanessa Gordon's wearing? The same shirt as me. This exact same shirt. We look like idiots. I think I'm gonna have to go home at lunch and change. I may go now. What's this?"

She reads the sign and gets super-excited. "Oh, David Nelson!" she says. "He's got the same lunch as me. You know him, right? He's that new kid? Just a sophomore? Totally hot? Totally hangs with the popular kids. God, he's gorgeous. You know who he is, trust me."

I try not to roll my eyes too much. Yes, I do know who David Nelson is, and, yes, he is totally hot, and totally hangs with the popular kids, but, unlike Becky, I don't care so much about that. What I'm wondering is if I could actually do it. Actually make the band.

Down at the bottom of the sign are these dangly things with a phone number, so I rip one off, then we head to Math.

"Ohmigod, I should go, too!" Becky is saying. "I should tell Ginger and Patty. I don't care about the band thing, I just want to meet David Nelson. What do you think his house is like? I bet it's nice. God, he's so fine! I bet all the popular kids will be there."

She keeps talking, but I'm not really listening. Becky and I used to be best friends but I don't feel as close to her these days. Not as close to anyone, really. Not since Mom died.

Could this band give me that? Give me something to care about again? Something fun? Something new? Lord knows, I need something.

As we walk down the crowded halls, Becky jabbering on about who-knows-what, all I can think about is that little slip of paper in my pocket. The rest of the day, through Math, Science, lunch, whatever... I sleepwalk through it all, completely zoned-out on thoughts of rock bands, my mom's bass, and David Nelson's phone number.

Do I have the guts to do this? Call him? Teach myself bass? Audition for a band?

Mom would want me to do this.

I think.

Would she?

I don't know.

And Dad? God... who knows what he wants anymore?

But I want it. I know this without any doubt. I want it. So, God help me, I'm just gonna have to find the courage to do it. Starting now.

Chapter 2

Okay, so it's after school and I'm down in the basement with my mom's bass. It's still in the same spot it was the day she died. You'd think after six months somebody would have moved it, put it in the storage room, at least, but I guess Dad and I just didn't have the heart or something.

I've got the case in my lap, wiping off a layer of dust, then I open it and pull out the old green Ibanez. It's the first time I've seen it since she died. It hurts to look at it. Hurts to hold it. I sit there for a minute or two, just thinking about Mom, letting the demons close in on me again. I wish I could say I was past this, but I'm not.

Still, after a minute or so, I clear my throat, wipe my

eyes. Got to carry on, right?

The bass. The green bass. I've always liked the color. Kind of dark, but not forest green. Sort of olive-y, but darker. Maybe I like the color because it's so hard to define.

Mom's black Peavey amplifier is right there, too, but I don't bother turning it on and plugging in. I know I'm gonna suck, so silent is probably better. Plus, if Dad comes home from work while I'm playing, I'd rather he didn't hear anything. I don't think he'd take it well. I'm not 100% sure about this, but still... better to keep it a secret for now. I think.

Sitting on the basement couch, I try to play a little, slowly and carefully pressing down on the strings, trying to remember what Mom showed me, wincing at how much it hurts my fingers. With my right hand, I plunk on the thick metal strings. With my left, I try to press them down on the fretboard. That makes it sound easy, but trust me, it isn't. You don't realize how tender your fingertips are until you try to play a bass guitar. If the strings were thin, soft, and smooth, it might be okay, but they're not. They're the exact opposite – thick, hard, and ribbed. It's like they're designed to cause you pain. Plus, my fingernails are getting in the way. I'm gonna have to cut them.

So anyway, I sit there on the couch for awhile, just trying to do anything. I can't play a song, of course, but I can sort of move my fingers around like Mom used to.

I can try and pluck the strings right. It's not music, to be sure, but with a lot of pain and finger-stretching, I manage to hit a few notes that ring clear. One or two. In between all the messy noise.

From up above, I hear my dad coming in, so I put the bass away and head upstairs.

"Hi, Dad," I say, walking into the kitchen. He's sitting at the kitchen table, eating something and looking exhausted.

"Oh, hey, Maggie." He sounds tired. No surprise there. "I picked up some Chinese on the way home. You hungry?"

"A little." I sit and open one of the white take-out boxes. "How's it going?"

"God, don't even ask. I'm so tired right now. I don't know how I get through the day sometimes."

"What's the matter?" I ask, starting to eat.

"Jesus, what isn't?" He leans back in his chair, shoulders slumped and eyes closed. "Those assholes, excuse my language, they're like vultures, just waiting to swoop down on me. Don't ever get a job like mine, sweetheart. All day long I'm on edge. I've gotta dot every i, cross every t, make a copy for every dumb shit in the company, excuse my language, and they're all waiting for one little mistake." He sighs heavily, then gives me a little smile. "I'm sorry, baby. You shouldn't have to listen to this. How are *you* doing?"

Through a mouthful of sweet and sour pork, I try to smile. "Pretty good, I guess."

"Do anything special at school today? Wait, how would your mom put it? '*Learn* anything special at school today?'"

We both laugh a little, remembering Mom, but then the room turns sad, just like always. I hate talking about her with Dad. You can just see the sadness wash over him, each and every time. As much as I miss her, he's a thousand times worse. He's just a shell of who he used to be.

"No, nothing special," I say. I've decided not to bring up the band. Not now, at least. "Just a regular ol' day at North Sycamore High. Fun, fun, fun, all the time."

Dad's leaning forward now, his eyes closed, chin resting on his fist. He looks a thousand years old. "You're a good girl, Maggie. I'm proud of you. Your mom would be, too."

We're silent for awhile. Me eating, Dad's chin still on his hand, eyes still closed. He occasionally sips from his glass of scotch. "Oh, I just remembered," he finally says. "You're not gonna like this, but I'm not gonna be able to send you to that thing next spring. The Florida thing. We just can't afford it."

"What? But, Dad! You promised!" It's this week-long trip to Florida the school's Spanish club is putting on. "Everyone's going! *Everyone*!"

"Don't start in on me," he says, opening his eyes and picking up his fork. "You think I like this? Telling you you can't do stuff? I hate it." He shovels some kung pao chicken into his mouth and starts chewing.

"But, Dad... I... You..." Dad's shaking his head and giving me this look and I know there's no point in continuing.

"Don't, baby. Just don't." He takes a sip of his scotch. "I would love to send you. I would love, love, *love* to send you. God knows, you deserve it. But I can't. I just can't."

I slump in my chair and sulk for awhile, picking at my food. Finally, "I know, Dad."

And there's nothing else to say, so we just eat. If Mom were still alive, I'd be able to go. It's as simple as that. There were two paychecks back then, so things were different. In every way.

Sitting there in silence, me eating, Dad drinking his scotch, my thoughts turn back to the bass downstairs. I know I'm gonna have to tell him about that eventually, but I really don't want to. You can see what he's like. Tired, sad, a little pissed off. Me pulling out the bass? Trying to be in a rock band? Looking just like Mom? I don't want to do that to him. I'll have to, eventually, but not tonight.

So we finish up the Chinese food, then clear it all away. We talk about nothing in particular, just stuff. Safe stuff. He finishes his glass of scotch and fixes another. I know he'll finish that one, too, and make a third. It's how he deals with Mom's death, getting a little drunk every night. I hate it, but I guess I can't blame him. He's still my dad, right? He still goes to work every day, at a job he hates. He still keeps this roof over my head, still pays the bills, still buys the groceries. So he's sad. So he's drunk. It could be worse, right?

That's what I tell myself, at least, when it's bedtime and Dad's fallen asleep in the living room, the TV still on, the DVD of Mom's favorite movie still running.

It could be worse.

Chapter 3

Okay, so it's a couple days later and I'm sitting in the kitchen, trying to work up the courage to call David Nelson. I've been sitting here for like half an hour, actually, but still haven't done it. I've done a lot of other important things, though. Like staring off into space. Like eating some yogurt. Like putting the spoon in the dishwasher. A couple times I've dialed half of David's number, then stopped. That's always pretty impressive, I think. Now I'm staring at all the stuff on the refrigerator door. It's occupied me for quite awhile, actually. There's a lot up there.

For example, there's this big watercolor painting of a clown I did back in kindergarten. Dad was just crazy about that clown painting. Showed it to everyone. Said he'd gotten some calls from famous museums. They wanted to buy it from him for a million dollars, but he wouldn't sell it. Loved it too much.

There's a whole bunch of magnets up there, too, including this one shaped like the Eiffel Tower. Mom and Dad got that on their honeymoon to France. I wish I could go to France. Dad used to say he'd take me someday, but I doubt that's happening now.

Then there are these two photos that Mom loved so much. Dad had them blown up at some photo shop. One's a photo of her holding me in the hospital the day I was born. She looks happy and exhausted. I look like a beet. A beet with a pink hat.

The other picture's of Mom and Dad standing on the front steps of our house the day they brought me home. I look more like a sweet potato in that one, which I guess is an improvement. Mom and Dad look so happy. I think that's why Mom loved those photos so much. Not because I look like a root vegetable, but because she and Dad look so happy.

God, I miss Mom.

And Dad, too.

Because, let's face it, he pretty much died the same day she did. The old Dad, at least. The happy, energetic, sober Dad. His body's still around, but the rest of him's gone.

Sigh.

Deep, heavy sigh.

Okay, enough of that. Time to get some courage. Time to call David.

I don't know why I'm so nervous. Maybe because he's so gorgeous. I'm not all that good with boys. Cute boys, at least. I can talk to ugly boys just fine.

But, in truth, it's not just that David is crazy-hot. I'm mostly scared because I know I'm completely and totally faking my way through this. And what if he can tell? What if he starts asking me questions I can't answer? Like... I don't know... "What awesome songs can you play?"

Uh, none?

Or, "Who's your favorite bass player?"

I don't know *any* bass players. I don't know anything. I just have my mom's old bass. That's it. I mean, he's gonna figure this out eventually, but I'd rather he didn't do it on the first phone call.

I need this band. I really do. I know that sounds stupid, but it's true. A week ago, I'd never even considered being in a rock band. Now it seems like the only thing that'll fix my sad, pathetic life.

So I've finally dialed and the phone's finally ringing. My heart's racing, so I try to distract myself by looking at the tips of my fingers. They hurt like hell. It's all this practicing the last two days. I say "practicing," but it's more like Making Random Noises in the Hope Something Miraculous Happens. My left hand, the fingers are sore from pushing down on the strings. My right hand, the index finger is starting to get a blister from plucking the strings over and over. Plucking's not the right word. Thumping? Plunking? Anyway, it hurts like hell and there's a blister coming up. I guess I'll have to start using my middle finger. And if that one gets a blister, my ring finger. Then my pinkie. Then what? My thumb? My toes? Ridiculous.

Someone at David's house finally picks up and runs off to get him. Sounds like a teenager. Maybe a brother or a friend or something. He's probably got tons of friends. And a big house. They're probably having a party right now. On a Thursday.

"Hi. This is David."

I'm startled. Wow, David has a nice voice. A *sexy* voice. Hard to believe he's just a sophomore. "Oh! Hey! Hey, David." God, I sound like such a dope. "Um... this is, uh...this is... Maggie Blackman." Jesus, could I stutter any more? "You know, um... from school?"

There's a long pause. I thought he would say something, but he doesn't. I get nervous, wondering if I'm supposed to talk. I almost do, when finally, sounding annoyed, he says, "Okay."

This isn't going well. *Pull it together, Maggie!*

"So, um... I'm calling about the band."

"What do you play?"

"Bass?" I make it sound like a question. *Damn it, Maggie! Sound confident! He can tell!*

"Okay, fine," he says. "There's gonna be a lot of bass players trying out, but whatever. Can you play 'Wild Thing?'"

"Yeah, sure." Complete lie, of course. I don't even know what "Wild Thing" *is*. A song? "I can do that."

"Good. It's a dumb song, I know, but it's easy. If people can't play that, then hell with 'em."

"Yeah," I say, trying to sound all cocky. "Definitely." Oh, man, this song *better* be easy.

David gives me a few details on the tryouts – time, place, etc. – then hangs up.

I stand there in the kitchen, completely exhausted. But I've done it. I'm officially going to auditions. I have eight days to learn this so-called "easy" song. Hopefully well enough to fool David Nelson.

My heart's racing and I'm exhausted, but I can't help but smile. Things are happening. New things, exciting things.

I look at the photo of Mom and Dad standing on the front steps, holding their sweet potato. Maybe I'll be able to put a new picture up there soon. Something to make Dad smile again. His little sweet potato, all grown up and playing in a rock band.

Chapter 4

So I went online and got a copy of "Wild Thing." Been working on it ever since. I'd love to tell you I've mastered it, but I'm not even close. I guess the song's kind of simple, just like David said, and he's definitely right that it's stupid, but regardless, it's still hard for a newbie like me.

It's Monday, by the way. I'm at school, walking from Science to English, the halls crowded and noisy. Becky used to make this walk with me, but not anymore. I guess she's found other people to walk with. Cooler people.

As I walk, I absently feel the tips of my fingers. They're sore and tired and just want to be left alone. I hear someone call my name and look over and it's this guy named Damian Shaw.

"Hey, Maggie. You got a second?"

I don't really know Damian all that well, so I can't imagine what he wants. He's just this guy I kind of know. He's a junior, like me. I think he was in one of my classes last year. "I guess so. What's up?"

"Listen," he says. "I was wondering if you've ever thought about going out for the girls basketball team."

It's all I can do not to roll my eyes. I'm so sick of people asking me if I play basketball. It's annoying. And rude.

Oh, this would probably be a good time to tell you: I'm six feet tall.

Yeah, I'm a giant. Have been all my life. I hate it.

In fourth grade, I was taller than my teacher. Fourth grade! For a long time, I was taller than every boy I knew, which pretty much ruled out having a boyfriend. What boy wants to date Sasquatch?

Now, in high school, a few of them have caught up with me, thank God. I wish there were more. And I wish they were *taller* than me. My dad's taller than me. I wonder what it would be like to date someone who's really tall? I bet it would be great. I'd have to stand on my tiptoes when I kissed him, just like the perfect little elf girls in the movies. I want to be a perfect little elf girl.

To be honest, there's not much about my appearance I like. I'm way too tall, obviously. My boobs are too small. I'm pale and freckly. I guess I'm not fat, so that's nice. And my hair's not so bad. Long, shiny. I wouldn't mind a little curl in it. And the brown's kind of boring. Okay, I guess my hair sucks, too. But I'm tall, which is all Damian cares about right now.

Through narrowed eyes, I say, "No," then turn and start down the hall again.

"Wait, wait," I hear him say. He's catching up to me, pushing his way through the crowds. "I wasn't trying to be funny. It was a serious question. I think you should go out for the team."

"Leave me alone, Damian. I'm not a jock." I squeeze through a knot of people waiting to get into a locked classroom, leaving Damian behind.

Or did I? A few seconds later, there he is again. "Slow down, would you?" he says. "I want to talk."

I stop and face him. I give him my best *I-have-better-places-to-be* look. "Fine. Talk. But I only have a second."

You're probably wondering right now why I'm being so rude to this guy and, to be honest, I sort of agree with you. What is my problem? I guess someone asking me about my freakish height automatically puts me in a bad mood, but it's more than that, really. Lately, I'm always in a bad mood. Ever since Mom died, really. And Dad started changing. And I started losing all my friends because I'm changing, too.

So here I am, looking at Damian and all these thoughts are racing through my head and I realize with a shock that my eyes are starting to well up and if I'm not careful I'm going to start crying right here in the hallway. Jesus, I'm a basket case. *Focus, Maggie! Focus!*

I blink a few times, force myself to stop thinking about me, and instead concentrate on Damian. Like I said, I don't really know him, but he was in a class with me last year. Art class, I think. He's a nice enough guy. Decent-looking. He's tall, I'll give him that. What is he, like six-three? One of the few boys taller than me. He's actually kind of cute, now that I look at him. I decide to take the angry look off my face.

"Okay, so here's the thing," he says. "I'm on the basketball team, right?"

I didn't know this, actually, but I'll take his word for it. I couldn't care less about sports.

"And we practice every day right next to the girls team. So they're like family, almost. Plus, a lot of times, we travel together on the bus, going to play the same school, right?" Damian's talking really fast now, like he's worried I'm going to rush off. "Okay, so my point is, I care about the girls team. I want them to do well. And they're not. They're suckin'. They haven't won a game all year. They haven't even been close. They're awful. And so I thought, what can I do to help these guys? And that's why I'm here, talking to you."

"Because you think I could help the team."

"Exactly!" He smiles at me like I'm the smartest kid in class.

"Okay, Damian, I hate to break this to you, because I can tell you really do care about the girls team, and that's sweet and all, but I can't play basketball. I can't play any sport."

"You can't play *now*," he says, "but I bet you could. Look at you, you're made for basketball. You've got those great arms and those great legs and –"

Damian stops suddenly, realizing what he's said, and starts to blush.

This makes me flustered, too – *a boy likes my legs!* – but I say, "Well, you've never seen me play basketball. I'm awful."

"You'd get better. I could work with you. We could practice all the time. It'd be fun. We could hang out."

He's bright red now and, almost like it's a natural response, I'm blushing, too. Like crazy. Is he... what's going on here? Is this about basketball or is this about something else? I really can't tell. I just know I'm overheating and I'm going to be late for class.

"I'm sorry, Damian, but I've got to go."

"Will you think about it?"

"Yeah, sure," I say, though I know I won't. I've got this band thing to worry about.

But as I race into English class at the last second, I realize that maybe I shouldn't ignore it completely. Maybe the basketball team would be just like the band. A distraction. An escape.

And, anyway, how cute was Damian back there? Honestly, that's probably the sweetest way anyone's ever asked me to play basketball. I didn't feel like a freak at all. I felt almost... I don't know... cool.

And you heard him, right? Great legs. He said I have great legs.

Chapter 5

Okay, so it's Wednesday. I've been working on "Wild Thing" for six days now and have sorta maybe got it down, but I'll keep at it until auditions. David said there would be a lot of bass players there, so I've got to be good.

One of the "bass players" is Becky. I put that in quotes because it's two days to the audition and she still hasn't picked up a bass. I'm not sure she's even *seen* one, which is why I'm making her come to my house.

"You know I don't care if I make the band, right?" she says as we get off the school bus, backpacks on our shoulders. She's all pissed off that I'm making her do this. "I'm just going to see David Nelson."

"Yeah. You've made that clear. I just don't want

you embarrassing me."

"It's *you* who's going to be embarrassing," she says. "Nobody's taking this seriously, you know. Just you. And maybe some boys, but who cares? Why can't you just relax? Enjoy it? We're going to see this totally hot, totally popular boy. At his house, no less."

I feel like there's something I should say to this, but I don't know what it is, so we just keep walking. I never know what to say these days. To Becky, to anybody. I'm just this silent, moody, six-foot tall dumbass.

I used to be cool. I swear. I was funny and sweet and full of life. I had lots of friends and we'd all get together at someone's house and we'd make popcorn and listen to music and read magazines and talk about boys and laugh. It was all so easy back then.

Now? I can't do any of that stuff anymore. I've tried, but I just can't. I don't know how anymore.

So I don't say anything. And we're walking. It's only a block and a half from the bus stop to my house. Yeah, I still take the school bus, and, yeah, I've got my driver's license, but don't make fun of me. Ever since Mom died, Dad's nervous as hell about letting me drive. One more way my life is crap – I turn sixteen right after my mom dies in a car wreck.

Erm... I guess that sounds bad. Trust me, having my mom die is way worse than not being allowed to drive. *Way* worse. But never being able to drive is sort of like an added insult, you know? Like, one more way for God to stick it to Maggie Blackman.

Although it's not like we've got a second car for me to drive, anyway. Not since the crash.

"So, I know Ginger's trying out," Becky says as we approach my house. "And Patty. And Jennifer Salk. And I'm pretty sure Melissa Chang and maybe Julie Moreno. And I think Sarah Levy, but I think she's trying out for guitar, I have no idea if she can actually play. And maybe Kathy Lundquist."

"Are any boys trying out?"

"Who cares? I'm just worried about Jennifer Salk. She's that skinny freshman girl. You know, the blond one? Looks like a little plastic doll or something? All the boys think she's hot. They're so typical."

"Becky, could you please try and take this just a little seriously? I don't want David to think I'm just another stupid girl trying to impress him."

"Fine, fine. Jeez." She rolls her eyes and huffs. "You're no fun at all anymore."

I don't defend myself because I know she's right. And anyway, we've made it to my house.

We go down into the basement and I show her how to hang the bass around her neck, how to hit the strings with one hand, press them against the frets with the other. I show her how "Wild Thing" goes, then let her try to play along with the song. Her fingers are so weak and soft, she can't really make the notes ring true. It's mostly just a bunch of noise. Muffled thumps, clicks, and buzzes. Nothing even close to a song. Maybe if we stayed at it for a few hours we could get it sounding halfway decent, but I can tell Becky just wants to leave, and to be honest, that's fine with me. Our friendship is... well, I'm not sure you can even call it a friendship anymore.

So she leaves and I stay in the basement, going through the song a few times, thinking about how I don't have any friends, wondering if I'll ever be fun again, marveling at how much stronger my fingers have gotten in just a week or so, and wondering if I *actually* sound good or if I just sound good compared to Becky.

From up above, I hear Dad coming in, so I put away the bass and head upstairs.

And no, I haven't told him about the band thing yet and, yes, I feel guilty, but come on, give me a break. Any day I can have a normal, sober, relatively happy father, I consider myself lucky. I'm not going to do anything to screw that up. Not intentionally, at least.

When I get to the kitchen, he's standing at the counter looking at some mail. He's already made himself a scotch on the rocks. Awesome.

"Hi, Dad," I say, giving him a kiss on the cheek.

"Hey, baby," he says, sounding tired. "How's it

going?"

We chat about nothing for awhile, but it's nice and reminds me of the old days. There are some bills in the mail, and he complains about that a little, but it's no big deal. For the most part, he's my good ol' dad and I love him. We make spaghetti together and I tell him about school. He talks about some big important basketball game he wants to watch but, like I said, I don't really care about sports. I pretend I do, though, because it's nice talking with him.

When the spaghetti's boiling and there's nothing to do, he takes his scotch into the next room and turns on the TV. I sit in there with him, but he's watching some kind of sports news so I don't really pay attention. Instead, I think about "Wild Thing" and whether I'm ready for the auditions and whether I'm gonna suck just a little or suck a whole bunch. I daydream a little, imagining myself making the band and how cool I'd be and how everyone would want to be around me and tell me how great I am and all the boys would think I'm hot and life would be perfect, forever and ever.

Then I look over at Dad and feel guilty about keeping all this a secret from him. Right now it's only been a week or two, but what if I *make* the band? Ridiculous, I know, but what if I do? What if months pass and I'm practicing all the time and I *still* haven't told him? I'm still sneaking around, keeping it all a secret? That sounds awful.

"Um, Dad?"

He gives me a grunt from his easy chair, still watching his sports news.

"What was it like when Mom was in a band?"

That gets his attention. He looks at me suspiciously. "What do you mean?"

"Well, I don't know. Was it, you know... cool? Was it fun?"

He still looks a little annoyed and takes a sip of scotch, but then stares off into space for a bit and his face relaxes.

"Yeah. Yeah, it was fun." He looks at me again. "But she was just a kid. High school, college. It wasn't serious or anything. Just for fun." He drains his glass, pulls himself out of his easy chair, and heads into the kitchen for a refill. "She was pretty good, too. The band was nothing special, but your mom was good. And she was super-cool up there on stage. So, yeah. It was fun to watch."

I follow him halfway, leaning against the door frame there between the kitchen and the den. He's fixing himself a new drink and I'm wrestling with guilt. "Do you... um... Do you think that's... I don't know... something I should try?"

He gives me a sharp look. "What? Playing in a band?"

"Yeah. Maybe playing Mom's bass."

He sighs and looks pissy. "Jesus. That would be fuckin' weird. Excuse my language."

"Weird?"

"Yeah. Weird." He's got his new scotch on the rocks and takes a deep swallow. This conversation was a mistake. I think I'm just giving Dad an excuse to get drunk. "You? Holding your mom's bass? Fuck that. Excuse my language. I mean, you look just like her. If I had to see you playing her bass, too? I think I'd want to put a fuckin' bullet in my head."

And then he turns up his glass of scotch and drains the whole thing. Right in front of me. And then immediately starts making a new one.

I feel like I've been punched in the stomach. *Put a bullet in my head?* What am I supposed to do with that?

"Oh," is all I can say.

When Dad's glass is full, he starts back toward his easy chair and his sports. "But you do whatever you want, sweetie. What the fuck do I know? Excuse my language."

I stand there for a few miserable moments, then head up to my room. Christ, what a nightmare. My dad's gonna get friggin' *wasted* tonight. He's gonna sit down there and think about my mom and how she was in rock bands and how he wants to *die*. And, this time, it's completely my fault. Well done, Maggie. You just had to open your stupid mouth.

You know all those movies where there's this kid, and maybe her mom's died or run off or something, and her father's a mess, but the kid's really got her act together? It's like *she's* the adult? She's the wise one, the one who knows all the right things to say, the one who keeps everyone on course? You know those movies?

Why can't I be like that? Why can't I be wise and together and always know the right thing to say? Because I don't. I'm never like that. Ever. I'm just some goddamn kid, trying to do the best she can. And usually failing.

Fuck those movies. They're nothing like real life. Real life sucks.

Chapter 6

Becky's mad at me right now. She was going on and on about cute boys and rival girls and what we should do at David's house to get noticed and so on, forever and forever, and I thought I was gonna puke, so I interrupted her and started grilling her about "Wild Thing" and whether she could play it and she didn't care and I didn't care, so now we're driving in silence. Which is fine. She's sick of me, I'm sick of her, whatever.

It's Friday, by the way. We're heading to the auditions. I'm driving, which is a minor miracle. It's dark and cold and drizzling, so I figured no way would Dad let me drive, but he did. I told him we're going to a movie. I had to sneak the bass out to the car when he wasn't looking.

As I drive – not talking to Becky – I think about what she said. Not about competing with the other girls, but when she said I was taking this too seriously and should just relax and enjoy myself. So now I'm driving us out towards David's neighborhood, wondering if she's right. I'm definitely stressed out, that's for sure. I haven't been able to think of anything else all day. Is this good? Or am I over-doing it? I'm almost certainly *not* going to make the band, so why not just be like Becky, try to get in with the popular kids and enjoy the evening? I take a deep breath, then let it out slowly. *Relax, Maggie. Just have fun. You deserve a fun night, so have one.*

David lives in this really nice neighborhood, full of big giant houses. Why are the good-looking people always rich and the rich people always good-looking? It's not fair.

My phone's giving me directions as we drive, the road dark and shiny in the rain, but even if I didn't have GPS, it's pretty obvious which house is David's. Cars are everywhere. Parked in the driveway, on the street, down the block. It's like our entire school has shown up.

"There's Ginger's car!" Becky says. "And Patty's! Hurry up and park. I don't want to give them all a head start. Actually, just let me out."

I let Becky out, she runs up to David's house, and for some reason it strikes me as significant. Becky racing off to be with the cool people, leaving me behind.

Or maybe I'm reading too much into it.

Eventually, I find a place to park and I grab my bass and start walking toward David's. He said not to bring an amplifier, thank goodness, or I'd be lugging that big ol' thing, too. The bass is heavy enough.

I ring the bell and this very pretty woman answers and sends me down into the basement. As soon as I start down the stairs, the noise is overwhelming. And it's definitely not music. It's noise. Drums and cymbals are being randomly hit, multiple guitars are playing multiple songs. It's awful.

Down at the bottom, I see that David's basement is nothing like mine. It's gigantic, for starters. Like, three or four times bigger. Plus, it's just *nicer*. It's well-lit and has nice carpet. There's a pool table way over on the other side, plus some kind of bar or something. And for this one night, at least, it's completely packed with high school kids.

And when I say high school kids, what I mostly mean is high school *girls*. They're everywhere and they're all talking loudly and shrieking about God knows what and I can tell that Becky was right about nobody taking this seriously. I see a few girls I know, like Ginger and Patty, two of my old "friends," plus some girls I know only by reputation, like Jennifer Salk, who's over on the other side of the room, leaning against a post, batting her eyes and looking like a Barbie doll. She's short and blonde and pretty – basically everything I wish I was. I've never spoken a word to her but I hate her guts, just on principle.

There are a bunch of boys here, too, though none that I know too well. There's a guy setting up his drums who looks familiar. I think he's a senior. As I'm watching, he starts yelling at this other kid, but I can't tell why. There's a third kid over there, beating on drums and cymbals, making a huge racket. I wish he'd stop. This place is making my head hurt.

There are guitarists and bassists everywhere, some of them plugged into amplifiers and adding to the noise. Everything about this place confuses me. It's crowded and noisy and I need to slow down and figure out what to do.

Over by the pool table, I see a boy with a bass, so I head towards him. I recognize him from school, but I can't think of his name. He's plugged in and playing his bass. He's good. Better than me.

"Is this your amp?" I yell at him over the noise.

"No," he yells back, not bothering to stop his playing. "They told me to leave it at home. I don't know whose this is."

"Can I use it?"

He shrugs and keeps playing. He's a *lot* better than

me and my heart sinks. I don't have a chance.

As I set down my case and start pulling out my bass, I finally see David Nelson.

Damn, he's hot.

I guess at this point I should probably try and describe him for you. God, where to start? He's got the great cheekbones, of course. The jawline. The eyes, so dark brown they're almost black. The dark shaggy hair always falling in his face. The perfect skin, pale like mine, only on him it looks beautiful, not gross. Beneath his t-shirts and jeans you can see he's got strong arms and big, strong hands, like he plays his piano for hours.

God, what I'd do to go out with a boy like him.

Right now, he's walking around the room trying to organize things. He looks kinda flustered, actually. He talks to a boy with a guitar and points over toward the rest of the guitars, like "go over there" or something. Then he's yelling at that drummer kid to quit playing. Then he's answering some question from one of the girls and I can tell just from his expression that it has nothing to do with music and he's getting even more annoyed. Then he's talking to the other drummer, the older guy, who looks kind of pissed off about something, and David looks kind of pissed off, too, and tries to tell him something, but the guy doesn't look any happier. And then that same girl from before – it's Julie

Moreno, by the way – is talking to him, clearly about something stupid, and I realize that she's just following him everywhere, flirting with him and thinking she's so special. David tries to ignore her and goes over to some guitarists and tells them something, but of course, Julie's still following him, trying to be all flirty and cute, and I'm watching all this while I pull out my bass and plug it in and I can tell that David is starting to get really annoyed because nobody's doing what he wants them to do and Julie won't shut up and then he's walking over to *me*.

"How many basses have we got?" he asks me.

I have no idea what to say to this. I mean, I suppose I could say *something*, but I literally can't say *anything*. I'm just frozen, standing there looking at this Greek god, my mouth hanging open and drool dripping off my chin. I'm so pathetic.

"...but then I was thinking that maybe you'd already seen that movie..." This is Julie, who's still following him around, still yapping. "...and wouldn't want to see it again, but you probably like action movies. You do, don't you? I bet you do. Because I like them, too, you know, but I like funny movies, too. Have you seen..."

And so on.

"Are you two the only bassists?" David asks the boy there with me, looking *really* annoyed. "I thought I saw... Jesus, where are they? Fuck. You two, stay here."

And then he's storming off, Julie right behind him.

"Man, he looks pissed, doesn't he?" It's the boy next to me and this sort of breaks me out of my daze.

"Yeah. I guess he does."

"So," the boy says to me over all the noise, still playing his bass, "you been playing for long?"

I'm about to answer when I hear somebody shouting, "Jesus Fucking Christ would you just SHUT UP?!?"

I look over and see that it was David Nelson. Actually, everybody is looking at him. The room's gone almost silent.

"Why don't *all* of you shut up?!?" David says, looking around the room, completely furious. "Can you do that?!? Can you just shut the fuck up?!?" He's standing there in the center of the basement, his face red and sweaty. He looks like he's ready to kill somebody. Anybody. *Every*body.

The whole room's looking at him now, but he's just standing there, crazy-eyed. After maybe five seconds of silence, he storms up the stairs, and slams the door at the top.

"Whoa," the boy next to me says under his breath.

I'm inclined to agree with him. Whoa, indeed.

Chapter 7

The basement feels like a totally different place, now that it's silent. Everyone's just sort of wide-eyed, looking at each other. Eventually, a few people start whispering. There's a big clot of girls over on the other side of the room and they start talking quietly. Becky's with them. Julie Moreno's still standing in the center of the room, looking shell-shocked, but then she stumbles over to the other girls.

"So, what now?" It's the other bass player, talking super-quiet. I remember his name now. It's Ty. He's a senior. "Do you think the auditions are over?"

I shrug. How would I know? It's the first audition I've ever been to. Maybe they're all like this.

Mom knew about auditions. She went to them when

she was my age. I wish I could've asked her.

People are starting to talk a little now and the room's getting louder, but it goes silent again when we hear the basement door open and David comes stomping back down. Only this time he's got a couple guys following behind him. One of them looks like he must be David's father, but the other guy's someone I know, a kid from my History class named Austin.

And now that I think about it, Austin's last name is Nelson, so he must be David's older brother. They don't really look much alike, though. Austin's not super-hot. He's a lot taller, though.

"Okay, everybody!" David is standing in the center of things, both hands raised. "Listen up and don't start talking, okay? Just listen!" He still looks a little crazy, his face all red and sweaty. He's not nearly as gorgeous like this. "I thought I could do this with just me, but *clearly* we're gonna need to split things up! So just shut up for a second and listen!" He pauses for a breath. "If you're a guitarist, you're going to be with my brother, Austin!"

"Don't go over now!" David's father says, raising his hand. He's gray-haired and balding and looks more like Austin than David. "Don't even move. Just wait 'till David is done, then go over to Austin. All guitarists."

Back in the center, David is still wild-eyed. Maybe a little better. "Bass players. You're gonna be with my dad."

"That's me!" his dad says, walking over toward me and Ty, his hand in the air. "I'll be over here." He's standing right next to me now. "Don't come over yet! Just wait."

"Drummers!" David says. "I'll handle you, I guess."

There's quiet then and everybody's watching David. He's looking around the room with intense eyes. It's almost like one of those movies where the hero is surrounded by bad guys and he's sizing them up, trying to figure out who to attack first.

Standing beside me, Mr. Nelson watches. He looks vaguely nervous. I'm starting to think David has a bit of an anger problem.

"Okay," David says, still eyeing everyone, hands raised, ready to fight. "When I say go, you can head over to your people. But *don't* start talking. No screaming, no jabbering, no nothing. Just go over. And once you're there, just shut up and wait. You think you can handle that? Think you can shut up and wait?"

From next to me, Mr. Nelson says, "Easy, son."

David looks at his dad real quick, then back at the room. "Okay. Everybody ready? Go."

There's a bunch of action then, but nothing like before. No madness. Just people moving around, all of them quiet and intimidated.

As expected, the largest group by far is the bass players. And, no surprise, it's mostly girls. In fact, the only boys there are Ty and this skinny sophomore kid I've only seen a few times before. Everyone else is girls. And only one of them has a bass. Well, two if you count me. The other bass is around Kathy Lundquist's neck. I have no idea if she can play, but I'd be willing to bet none of the other girls can. Becky sure can't.

"Alright, bass players, listen up." It's Mr. Nelson. He has a calm voice and warm, friendly eyes. I instantly like him. "Obviously, we'll only need one bass player at a time, so we need to figure out who's going when. Also, you can use this amp right here, so if you brought your own, don't bother. And... I think that's it. So. Let's figure out who's going first."

With a smile, he closes his eyes, spins in a circle a couple times, and points. When he opens his eyes, he's pointing at Melissa Chang. "Congratulations!" he says. "You're our lucky winner!"

The rest of us are told to find somewhere out of the way, which isn't easy with such a big crowd. I'm lucky and get a spot on one of the couches. It's leather and really comfy.

In the center of the room, things are starting to take shape. Melissa Chang is standing there with Kathy Lundquist's bass around her neck, acting like she's not nervous, but I can tell she is. David Nelson is sitting at an upright piano, which is turned sideways so he can see everyone. He looks impatient and still a little scary. Some freshman boy I don't know is over on the drum kit and John Knowlson is on guitar. I know John a little because he lives in my neighborhood and rides my bus. He's older than me, a senior, but he's always seemed like a nice guy.

David has a microphone over at his piano and he keeps saying stuff like, "Are we ready?" or "Let's go, let's go, let's go." He's saying it into the mike, so it comes out of the speakers really loud. Finally, when everyone's set, he counts them off, 1, 2, 3, 4, and they start.

It's horrible.

No, seriously, it's *horrible.* It's almost painful to watch, it's so bad.

Remember how I told you "Wild Thing" was a really easy song? Well, apparently it's not easy enough, because between Melissa Chang and that freshman kid on drums, I don't know if I've ever heard anything so bad.

Now, Melissa, that's no big surprise. I knew she couldn't play bass and, standing there in front of the whole room, she doesn't even try. She just kind of sways back and forth with the music, batting her eyes at David and trying to look sexy. Her hands are on the bass, but they never actually move. She's not trying to fool anybody.

The drummer, though? Dear Lord. When they first start the song... well, he *doesn't* start. He waits like half a second and *then* starts. And I guess he figures he needs to catch up because then he starts drumming super-super-fast. Way faster than the song goes. And then – I guess to make up for it – he slows down, super-super-*slow*. And then he stops altogether for a second or two, before starting again. I swear, all of this is true. It's ridiculous.

John Knowlson, on guitar, is actually doing a halfway decent job, but let's be fair, how good is he gonna sound when he's got this freshman drummer spazzing out and Melissa doing nothing at all? He's trying to help the other two, God bless him, counting out loud for the drummer, standing close to Melissa and showing her what notes he's hitting. She won't look at him, though. She's only got eyes for David.

Who, by the way, is freaking out. I'm watching it all from the couch and I don't know whether to laugh or run for my life. David's eyes are wide and his mouth is open and I'm amazed that his hands are still able to play the song, because every other part of him seems to be paralyzed with shock. First, he looks confused. Then horrified. Then angry.

He stops playing. John follows. The freshman kid keeps pounding for maybe ten seconds, then he notices and stops, too. Melissa, of course, never started.

The room is silent, everyone watching David. Waiting.

David doesn't speak. His eyes are closed and his forehead is resting against his microphone. Finally, sounding exhausted, he says, "Are you kidding me?"

Mr. Nelson says, “Take it easy, son.” He says it like he's talking to a wild dog, trying to convince it not to attack.

David doesn't acknowledge this. He just turns and glares at Melissa. He's definitely not a Greek god right now. Maybe the God of War. "Are you freakin' kidding me?"

Melissa tries to give him a sexy little smile but he just rolls his eyes disgustedly and turns away. Melissa's face crumples. She's dead to him. She knows it. We all do.

Turning to the drummer, David looks like he wants to scream at the kid. *Wants* to scream at him, but doesn't. He's gritting his teeth so hard I'm worried his jaw is going to explode. "That was.... That was..." He turns and looks at his dad. "What am I supposed to say to this idiot? That was the worst thing I've ever heard."

His dad immediately turns to the room and says, "Okay, everybody! We're gonna meet up in our groups again! Wherever you were before, go back there now, okay?"

Behind him, on the drum kit, the little freshman kid looks like he wants to cry.

I've got to tell you, this evening has taken a strange turn. David Nelson – the gorgeous, mysterious, perfect new boy – now seems dangerous. And not sexy dangerous, either. Scary dangerous.

"Okay, bass players!" It's Mr. Nelson. He's motioning for us to gather around him. "Come in close, everyone."

We're all in a bunch, then. Melissa's still got the bass on, looking shaken. I can't blame her.

"All right, guys," Mr. Nelson says to us in a kind, calm voice. "Obviously... that wasn't good. But don't worry, we'll fix this." He thinks for a moment and clears his throat. "Um... I guess I should start by asking... is there anyone else here who can't actually play?"

That would be over half the group, of course, but at first, no one raises a hand.

"No one's going to make you leave," Mr. Nelson continues. "But do you really want to get yelled at like this girl just did? Nobody wants that. So, be honest... who here can't play?"

Eventually, all the pretenders raise their hands and Mr. Nelson, still being kind, has them go find someplace around the periphery of the room where they can watch the rest of the auditions. There are only four of us left then: me, Kathy Lundquist, that senior Ty, and that sophomore boy, who tells us his name is Nick.

Mr. Nelson looks at me and says, "You ready to play?"

After seeing what Melissa just went through, I kind of want to say, *Hell no*, and run for the door, but I don't. I came here to change my life, so I might as well give it a try. "Sure."

My bass is leaning against the couch. I grab it, plug into the communal bass amp, take a deep breath, then turn to face my destiny. Or my downfall.

Chapter 8

You know how I said that David was so gorgeous and I'd do anything to go out with a boy like him? Forget all that. Because right now, standing there in the middle of the basement, a bass hanging from my neck, all I can think is, *Please don't let him go psycho on me.*

This time through the song, it looks like it's going to be me, a senior boy on guitar – I think his name is Josh – and another senior on drums – I think his name is Kieran. Something like that.

"Do you know how to play?" It's the guitarist, Josh, speaking quietly. He looks as scared as me.

"Sort of," I whisper back.

Clearly, this isn't what Josh wanted to hear, because

now he looks even more scared.

Over on drums, Kieran doesn't look scared. He looks angry. Kieran's the one who was yelling at the other drummers earlier.

Man, is this what bands are like? Is everyone psycho?

Standing there, surrounded by madness, I can feel myself falling apart a little. My heart's starting to race, my stomach feels like a bowling ball sinking to my feet, and against my will I start thinking about my mom. She'd gone through all this. She could have warned me.

Calm down, Maggie. Don't panic. Don't cry. Don't think about your mom.

"So how are you feeling?" It's Mr. Nelson, standing right there in front of me, right up close. He can tell I'm freaking out. "It's Maggie, right?"

I nod.

"Just relax, Maggie. You've got this."

I nod some more and breathe a few times, trying to calm myself.

"If you get lost," he says, "look at the other musicians. Just lock in on them, Maggie. You're all in this together."

Over the speakers, I can hear David talking into his microphone. "Are we ready? Come on, come on. Let's do this!"

Mr. Nelson winks at me as he walks away. I'm breathing and looking at the floor, my hands on the bass, ready to play. I'm sweating like a plow horse. *Watch the other musicians, watch the other musicians.* I look up at David. No, too scary. I look over at Kieran on drums. Nope. Still no good. Finally, I settle on Josh, the guitarist. He's looking at me, too. We're both terrified.

"Ready?" David says into the mike. "1, 2, 3, 4!"

Josh immediately screws up. I mean, instantly. There's this little guitar thing at the beginning of the song and he plays it, but everyone else in the band skips it, so he's completely off, and before the song even starts, it comes crashing down.

"Damn it!" David yells into the mike. "I said don't play that part! Didn't you hear me say that?"

Josh is shaking his head, terrified.

"Just skip the frickin' intro and go straight into the opening verse! Can you do that? Can you all just do that one thing?" He looking at me and Kieran now.

Kieran glares back at him. "I didn't mess it up," he says in a flat, aggressive tone.

"No, you didn't," David says, sounding just as annoyed. "Congratulations." They sound like they're ready to fight.

I didn't mess it up, either, but there's no way in hell I'm going to say so.

Turning his attention back to Josh, David says, "So, do you understand what I want? Skip the intro, start with the first verse."

Josh nods.

I wish I could tell you I'm feeling sorry for Josh right now, but I can't. All I'm thinking is, *I'm glad it's him getting yelled at and not me.* Isn't that awful?

David counts us off. 1, 2, 3, 4.

This time, we nail it. We roll into the song and my eyes are locked on Josh and he and I are hitting our notes at the same time and I'm vaguely aware that David is singing, but I truly can't hear it, I'm concentrating so hard. About halfway through the song, I feel like I'm doing pretty well, so I sneak a peek over at David. He's paying zero attention to his piano. His hands play on their own while he scans me and Josh and Kieran, watching us, judging us. He looks straight into my eyes and I completely miss the next two or three notes. In a panic, I look over at Josh again and get myself back in sync, matching my notes to his, and then I'm doing pretty good. And then, somehow, amazingly, the song's over.

I did it. I survived.

There's a bunch of confusion then as David calls for

new musicians to step in, so Ty's coming up and unplugging me from the amplifier, and I'm gathering my cord, and the drummer and guitarist are changing, too, so there's tons of noise and movement, and I'm kind of in a daze, to be honest, but I make my way back to the leather couch and sit down. I'm sweaty and exhausted and my heart is racing and I honestly can't tell if I want to start laughing or burst into tears.

Wow. What a rush.

The new musicians start playing then and, to be honest, sound pretty good. The drummer is maybe a little weaker than Kieran, and the guitarist is nothing special, but the bass player, Ty, is really, really good. He sounds like a pro. He's completely rock solid through the entire song, never missing a note, never losing his rhythm. In fact, I can see that the guitarist and drummer are both watching *him* as they play. Clearly, in this particular trio, Ty is the one holding everything together, and, trust me, that right there would be enough to kill my buzz for the evening, but then Ty's got to start throwing in all these fancy riffs, his fingers moving up and down the frets, never losing time, never messing up the song. How long has this guy been playing? Longer than two weeks, that's for sure. I'm screwed.

When they finish, David says his first positive thing of the night. "Outstanding," he says into the mike. Then immediately, "Okay, who's next?"

Lots of movement then as people trade places and get ready. Ty looks supremely confident as he unplugs and walks past me. He knows he's won this. I want to sink into the floor.

Okay, well, as you can imagine, the auditions keep moving forward. David keeps calling people forward and "Wild Thing" gets played over and over and over. Since there are only four bassists left, I get up there every fourth time. There are five guitarists, so they cycle through every... well, I'm sure you can do the math. David is constantly shifting people around, so every time I get up there to play, it's never with the exact same crew.

I have to say, though, as I get up there more and more, each time I'm a little less nervous. I can actually breathe. And look around. And listen to the song. I'd like to think that I'm sounding better, too, but you'd have to ask David Nelson about that.

And it's clear that he's already making decisions. For example, that first drummer? The one who sucked so bad? He only gets to play once more, then never gets called up again. Kathy Lundquist, she's not as bad as him, but she only gets up there three times. Apparently, that's all David needed to hear. Same for the other bassist, that sophomore named Nick. He's just as good as me, to be honest, but for some reason, David keeps calling me up, while Nick and Kathy stay off to the side. Crazy, huh?

But I need to be completely clear here: there's no way I'm winning. I mean, you just need to hear Ty. He's *great*. He plays like he's in college or something. He's just worlds better than me. So, even though it's awesome that David keeps calling me up there, I really can't explain it. Ty's the guy he wants. It's not even a hard decision.

You'd think this would have put me in a horrible mood, wouldn't you? But for some reason, it hasn't. I'm actually sort of happy. And you know what, I even think I know why. It's because this is the most fun I've had since... well, probably since before my mom died, back in May. I mean, I know earlier I was terrified, and, yeah, sure, David is turning out to be kind of a dick, but still, getting up there and playing, it's just *fun*. The drums, the guitar, the volume. The way it all just punches you in the chest over and over. I love it. Earlier, I was terrified to walk up there. Now, I can't wait for him to call my name. I bounce up there, ready to rock. It's totally addictive.

The woman who answered the door – I'm sure she's David's mom – comes downstairs then and she's got a bunch of cups and a pitcher of what looks like iced tea and she's going around and offering it up to people. She's super-pretty. I can tell it's from her that David gets all his hotness. David's dad is nothing special. He looks more like Austin. And just as I'm looking at them and thinking about that I'm interrupted by...

“Maggie! What are you doing here?”

I look up and who's standing there but Damian Shaw. Yes, *that* Damian Shaw. The same Damian Shaw who told me I had great legs. Who *may* have been flirting with me, I'm not sure.

"Damian? What are you doing here?"

"I asked you first."

"I'm here for the audition."

"Seriously? You're a musician?" Damian's kneeling down in front of the sofa so he's on my level and he's got this big smile on his face and he's looking at me like I'm just the coolest person in the history of the world and, well, I can't help it, I start grinning back at him like an idiot and I think I'm blushing, too, but I just can't help it. "I didn't know you played in a band," he says. "That's awesome!"

"Well, I'm not really in a band," I say, my face on fire. "I'm trying out for one. But what are *you* doing here?"

"Oh, I'm here picking up Austin. We're going downtown. We're on the basketball team together."

I look up, then, and Austin's left the guitarists and he's coming over towards me and he's got this girl with him who I sort of know named Audrey Gill.

"Hey, Maggie," she says. "What's up?" Audrey's a

junior, same as me, and we're in a couple classes together, but she is totally cool, way cooler than me. She's got a pierced nose and a pierced belly button and she wears cool thrift store clothes and every few weeks she dyes her hair a different color. Right now it's pink. "You in the band?"

"Erm... not yet." I'm too intimidated by her coolness to say much more, but I suddenly *really* want to make this band, just so Audrey Gill will think I'm cool.

"Well, good luck," she says, giving me a really nice smile, a smile someone as cool as her really doesn't need to give a nerd like me. I want to bathe in the warm light of her awesomeness.

She and Austin start walking off, and Damian says goodbye, too, and then they're all heading up the stairs and I'm sitting there on the couch with my head spinning, thinking how cute Damian is and how nice Audrey had been and how I wish I'd been a little cooler but the whole thing had been so unexpected and confusing and then, suddenly, Damian's *back*, and he's there next to me, kneeling down, looking nervous, and he says, "So, how much longer's this thing, anyway? Because, you know, Austin and I are going downtown. You could come with us. Audrey'll be there, so you'd have a girl to talk to."

My God. He's... Is he asking me out? He's not asking me out, is he? This is just him being friendly, right?

"I, um... I'm not really sure," I say.

Just then, as if he'd been planning it, David Nelson says into the mike, "Maggie. Back up here. John? Gene? You, too."

I look at Damian apologetically and he says, "Well, I guess not, then."

I stand and Damian stands and once again I appreciate how he's taller than me. "Sorry, Damian. But thanks anyway."

"Yeah, sure thing," he says, looking embarrassed and totally adorable. "Good luck with this, though. Seriously. Good luck!" And then he's heading up the stairs and I'm getting my bass and heading back over to the amplifier, my head absolutely swimming.

It turns out, I don't need my bass after all. David wants us to sing.

"I'm gonna play a melody," he says to about seven of us, all crowded around his piano, "and I want you to sing it back to me. John, we'll do you first."

So David plays five or six notes on his piano, then listens while John Knowlson, the guitar player, sings it back to him. It's a little weird at first, and I'm glad it's John going first and not me, but after a few minutes of standing there watching people sing, I've got a pretty good feel for it and I'm not nervous when David calls my name.

I don't know what melody David is playing on his piano – he's probably just making something up – but it's not too hard and I sing it back to him without too much trouble. He plays it a little higher, and so I sing that back to him as well. We go higher still and I mostly keep up, but then he plays it crazy-high and my voice cracks and everybody sort of laughs but I don't mind. I'm having fun.

The best part? When he gets around to Ty, the bass player who's so awesome, we learn that Ty can't sing a lick. I mean, he's *awful.* He tries, God bless him, but all his notes are either sharp or flat and his voice is strained and cracking. He clearly knows this and his face gets super-red and I feel really bad for the guy, but at the same time, it's the first time all night I've thought I might actually have a chance. Sure, Ty can play circles around me on bass, but maybe David wants a backup singer, you know? Maybe I've got a shot.

And that's pretty much how things end. David tells us he'll try to decide soon and then we're all packing up our stuff and leaving. Becky left about an hour ago with some of the other girls, so I don't need to drive her home. I just drive home through the dark, rainy night, my ears ringing from all the loud music, a big smile on my face. It feels like maybe my life is turning around a little.

But when I get back home and start walking toward the front door, bass in hand, I hear the stereo blasting inside. It's Dad, of course. Getting drunk and listening to Mom's favorite band. *Way* too loud.

Christ. Did any of those other kids have to go home to a drunk parent?

I stand there in front of the house, figuring out how to get in without Dad seeing the bass. I should've planned this out earlier.

There are bushes in front of our house. I suppose I could just hide the bass behind them for the night. Walk in without it. But I don't want to risk that. What if someone steals it?

I decide to walk around behind the house and see if the door going into the basement is unlocked. If it is, perfect. If it's not, then I'll just stash the bass back there somewhere, maybe behind the tool shed.

As I walk around the side of the house, I wonder if our neighbors hate us. I bet they do. I mean, the music is *blasting*. All the windows are shut, but I can hear it just fine, word-for-word. God, when did we turn into the neighborhood's weird family?

Back behind the house, heading for the basement door, I'm feeling pretty good about the plan. It's super-dark back here. I'd feel safe leaving the bass, but I'll check the back door anyway, just in case. If I'd planned this out better, I would have unlocked it earlier, but whatever. Maybe next time.

And just as I'm thinking that, the motion-activated floodlights come on, illuminating the entire back yard, plus me, standing there frozen, bass in hand, feeling like a total dumbass.

Now, if I were some kind of movie star or something, I'd probably sprint out of sight or dive into the woods or, I don't know, do *something* cool, but instead, I'm just frozen there. I think maybe I turn in a circle.

I don't know how much time passes while I stand there, but clearly long enough for Dad to notice, because up above, the sliding glass door opens and he comes walking out onto the deck.

"Who is that?" he yells.

He's drunk. He doesn't know it's me. Maybe I can run for it.

"Maggie? Is that you?"

Crap. I hold the bass behind me, trying to be all casual about it.

"Hi, Dad."

"What are you doing back here? What is that? What are you holding?"

Busted.

"What are you doing?" he yells. "What is that?" He's still yelling, slurring his words, drunk as hell.

Plus, now that the sliding glass door's open, the music's at full volume. Quite a show for the neighbors, eh?

I let him see the bass.

He's silent for a moment, the music still blasting, then says, "What the fuck is that?"

God, I wish I could just die. I start walking back around to the front of the house.

"Wait! What the fuck is that? Is that your mom's bass?"

I continue walking, thinking murderous thoughts. When I finally get to the front door and go inside, Dad's back in the living room, but I can see that the sliding glass door is still open, so the neighbors can still hear the music. Lucky them.

"What are you doing with that?" Dad says. He's swaying a little, scotch glass in hand.

"Dad, can we talk about this in the morning?"

"No. What the fuck are you doing?"

Right now, I hate my dad, fully and completely. That's a terrible thing to say, but it's true. "I'm trying out for a band! Is that a fuckin' problem?" I put the bass down, stomp past Dad into the living room, slam shut the sliding glass door, and turn down the music. "You listen to that too loud!"

"Don't talk to me like that," he says. "I'll listen to it

however I want. What are you doing with a band?"

"Trying out!" I'm yelling now, even though the music's quiet.

"Is that what all that shit was the other day? All that shit about your mom and her band?"

"Whoa, I'm surprised you remember, you're so drunk!"

"You need to watch that tone, Maggie!"

"Why should I watch *my* tone? You're the one who's drunk all the time! You should watch *your* tone!"

And then I storm past him, pick up the bass, and stomp up the stairs to my room. I slam my bedroom door, drop the bass, fall onto my bed, and start crying my eyes out. Down below, I hear the music come back on, louder than before.

I don't know how long I cry. It seems like hours, but it's probably not. Eventually, I clean myself up and get into bed. I can't sleep. Instead, I lie there in the dark thinking how much I hate my life and hate my dad. I think about how I'd been having such a fun night and then my dad ruined the whole thing. I think about how much I need to make David Nelson's band. So I can be over *there* all the time instead of here. So I can be around adults who actually *help* you, instead of just passing out drunk in the living room. So I can *make* the loud music, instead of just hearing it on endless repeat downstairs while I lie in my darkened bedroom, trying to fall asleep.

Chapter 9

So Dad and I are barely talking now. I slept as late as I could Saturday, hiding out in my room, hoping to avoid him. I laid in bed, thinking. Thinking about Dad and how he's ruining my life. Thinking about the tryouts and whether I'd been good enough. Thinking about Damian Shaw and how cute he'd been at David's house. Wondering if he'd been asking me out. Wondering if he liked me.

Eventually, hunger drove me out of my room and downstairs. Dad was gone. Beats me where he was, but he didn't come back until late. That's sort of the way Sunday went, too. He was probably avoiding me, which is fine. I didn't want to see him, either.

I spent a lot of the weekend playing bass. I went

online and watched some video music lessons, then went down into the basement and plugged into my mom's old amplifier for the first time. I'm happy to report it still works. Loud as hell, too. I was cranking songs on my Ipod and trying to follow along on bass, everything super-loud. I have no idea if Dad came in and heard me. I sort of hope he did. Fuck him.

It's Monday, by the way. I'm at school, sitting in English, waiting for class to start. I pass the time making a mental list of all the reasons David Nelson should pick me for his band:

1) I can sing, so that would let us do harmonies.

2) I'm a girl, so that might sorta add to the band's look, maybe.

3) I'm...

Well, okay, maybe there's only two reasons.

My mental list of reasons to pick Ty is even shorter. Just the one thing, really.

1) He kicks ass.

So I'm sitting here stewing, wondering if I can send psychic messages to David that bass playing is totally overrated, and singing ability is what he really needs to focus on. I don't think I'm having much luck.

So that's what I'm doing, waiting for the bell to ring, when Audrey Gill walks in and sits down right next to me.

"Hey, Maggie! How's it going?"

For a second or two, I'm silent, my mouth hanging open, thinking there must be some mistake, but then I manage to say, "Oh, hey, Audrey. What's up?"

Audrey's never sat with me before. We've got a couple classes together, but we're not friends. She's out of my league. She's all cool with the hipster kids and the emo kids. I don't know why she'd sit with a dork like me.

"That was so cool seeing you at Austin's house," she says, giving me a bright smile.

"Austin's house?" I say, completely flustered.

"Austin Nelson. My boyfriend. You know? Friday night?" She runs her fingers through her shoulder-length pink hair, looking so relaxed and confident.

"Oh, yeah," I say, laughing, desperate to seem cool. "Austin! The auditions!"

"So how did it go? Did you make the band?"

"I don't know," I say, suddenly eager, leaning across the aisle. "Do you know anything? Have you talked to David?"

"No," she says, pulling out a notebook and pencil. "I don't really know David all that well. He's kinda prickly. He hasn't called you?"

"No. I was..."

At that point, the bell rings, so I turn and look up toward the teacher. I barely hear her, though. I'm thinking about David Nelson. And Austin Nelson. And eventually, Audrey Gill.

Like I said, we're not friends or anything. She did come and sit next to me, though. And she's being totally nice. I'd love to be friends with her. She would instantly be my coolest friend. Actually, she'd be my *only* friend, the way things have been going. I saw Becky in the hall before class and she completely ignored me. She looked right at me, rolled her eyes, and starting talking to someone, like I wasn't even there. It was humiliating. I mean, I know we've been drifting apart, but she's not gonna go all "mean girl" on me, is she? We're not gonna be enemies, are we?

Well, anyway, I make it through English class and the bell rings. As we're gathering our books, Audrey says, "So. The band. Think you've got a shot?"

I tell her how it was really fun and how Ty was so much better than me, but how he couldn't sing and I could and she agrees that the singing thing can't hurt, but to be honest, she doesn't know what David is looking for, she doesn't know him all that well.

"I will say this, though," she says as we head out into the crowded hallway. "He may be kind of a dick, but he's an incredible musician. *Really* talented. I don't know if you could tell."

"Yeah, he seemed pretty good."

"He's *very* good. Austin plays guitar – he's got a little band-thingy with his friends – but he's not in David's league. Even he'll admit it."

I don't really know her boyfriend – they just moved to town this year – but I sort of want to say something, just to keep the conversation going. It's exciting, walking down the hall with a cool person. Maybe people will think we're friends. "So what did you guys do downtown? You and Austin."

"What, Friday? Not much. Got some pizza, wandered around for awhile. Austin called DeAndre, so we met up with him. You know DeAndre, right? We met up with him at Youngblood's. One of the girls behind the counter started hitting on Damian."

My heart jumps in my chest. "What? She was... Who?"

"Oh, just some chick. I can't remember her name. She goes to South Sycamore. She was *all about* Damian. It was kind of pathetic."

The bottom drops out of the hallway. I feel like I want to fall over. Damian? *My* Damian?

"What were they... What were they doing?"

We're at Audrey's locker and she's working the

combination on her lock. "Who? Damian and his little squeeze-toy? Oh, I don't know... stuff. She got off work and started following us around and I pretty much ignored them but they were kissing and everything. I wasn't really paying attention."

Okay, it's official. I like Damian Shaw. Big time. If I didn't, why would I feel like I want to die, right here in the hall? Why would I want to cry? Why would I want to kill this ugly, stupid, slutty South Sycamore High girl?

This is pathetic. I have no business feeling this way.

"So what are you doing after school?" Audrey says.

"Huh? What?" So smooth.

"You wanna get some coffee or something?"

Whoa. Well, *that* was a big shift of emotion. From devastation that some girl was making out with Damian Shaw to the utter amazement that Audrey Gill is asking me to have coffee with her. *The* Audrey Gill.

"Erm, yeah. I'd love that."

"Cool. We'll figure it out in Math. See you then." And then she's off, giving me a casual wave over her shoulder, her pink hair and hipster clothes disappearing through the crowd.

Wow. Audrey Gill waved to me in the hall. I

wonder if anyone saw?

Okay, well, anyway, I need to get to gym class, so I start heading in that direction, but before I get too far, this boy kind of pulls up next to me.

"Hey, Maggie," he says, and I look over and realize it's Josh, that guy from the auditions, the one who played guitar with me.

"Oh, hey Josh. What's up?"

"Oh, nothing much, just saying hi." He's walking along with me now. "Heard anything from David?"

"No. Have you?"

"No."

For some reason, I'm relieved to hear this. Maybe no one's heard. Maybe David hasn't decided. I still have a chance.

"So, it was fun playing with you," Josh says.

"Oh, yeah," I say. "Fun playing with you, too." I don't think I'll tell him he was the first person I'd ever played with.

"You're good," he says.

"Yeah. You, too. Wait. Really? You think I'm good?"

"Yeah," he says, completely earnest. "You're good. Better than me."

"Wow. Well, cool. Thanks, Josh."

"Sure. No problem." We walk in silence for a few seconds, then he says, "Okay, well, I guess I'd better get to class. Good to see you, Maggie!"

"Yeah, you, too. Later."

So he peels off and I keep going toward the gym, not entirely sure why he was talking to me. Lots of weird stuff happening today. Audrey Gill being totally nice to me, strange boys walking with me in the hall, acting like I'm all cool or something. And then there's the whole Damian Shaw thing. I'd rather not think about that.

As I walk, I realize that it's all about David Nelson's band. It's the only reason a girl like Audrey would want to hang out with me. It's the only reason random boys would want to talk to me in the hall. And it's the only way I could ever get a boy like Damian Shaw. Especially if he's got some horrible girl from South Sycamore High making out with him.

I *need* to make this band. Now more than ever. I need it.

Chapter 10

"I'm sorry, Maggie," David says on the phone, "but I've decided to go with Ty on bass."

Chapter 11

It's Sunday. I've hardly left my room all weekend. Hell, I've barely gotten out of bed.

David Nelson just *had* to call me on Friday. If he'd told me during the week, at least I would've had distractions. School to go to the next day. Homework. Audrey to hang out with. Something. Anything.

Instead, he tells me Friday afternoon, so my entire weekend is ruined. I've just been stewing. Miserable. Lying in bed, thinking about how my life is over, thinking about how they're probably having their first rehearsal this weekend, how they're all laughing and having fun and it's Ty over there rocking out when it should be *me*.

And I can't even call Audrey. I'm just not sure we're

good enough friends yet. I mean, we went to the coffee shop a couple times and that was great. And that vintage clothing store on Thursday, that was fun. But, still, it's only been a week, so are we *really* friends? Probably not when she finds out I didn't make the band. She'll dump me, go back to her old friends. The band's the only thing that made me cool. Now I'm just dumb ol' me again.

Actually, she probably already knows. She's probably over there right now, watching them rehearse. She's watching them kick ass and wondering why she ever thought I was cool.

There's a knock at my bedroom door and my dad's voice comes through. "Sweetie? Can I come in for a second?"

It's two in the afternoon and I'm still in my pajamas, lying there on my bed, staring at the ceiling. "Sure, Dad."

He looks hesitant coming in. I don't know what I look like. Hell, probably.

"I just thought I'd check on you," he says, standing there next to the door. "You've been kind of holed up for awhile. Everything okay?"

No, Dad. Nothing is okay.

"Yeah, Dad. I'm fine."

He nods and kind of stands there for a bit, rocking

back and forth a little, moving his lips in and out the way people do when they don't know what else to do. Finally, he says, "Um, listen... I was wondering..." He clears his throat. "I was hoping you might play the bass for me."

Well, *that* was completely unexpected.

"What do you mean?"

"Oh, you know. I was kind of an asshole before, excuse my language. I mean, I didn't really handle it well that time before. With the bass. I shouldn't have yelled at you like that. I'm sorry. I just... well... you know. So, I thought maybe I could listen to you now. If you're willing." He seems to run out of words then and just kind of looks around awkwardly.

"You want to hear me play?"

"Yeah. I would." He seems to be forcing himself to say this, but whatever. At least he's trying.

"Sure, Dad." And so I get the bass off the floor, take it out of its case, and sit with it on my bed. "What do you want me to play?"

"Anything. What can you play?"

"Not that much, really. I can play 'Wild Thing' for you."

"That would be great."

So I start playing it, sitting there on the edge of my

bed. It sounds stupid all alone, so I pull out my iPod and start the song up and play along with it. I'm not plugged into an amp, so you can't really hear the bass all that well, but still, I'm playing and Dad's listening, so that's something.

When I finish, Dad's real complimentary and asks if I can play anything else and I can't really, but there's this one song I've fooled around with a little, so I sort of try to fake my way through that and Dad says it sounds good and I tell him there's another song that maybe I could kind of play for him, but he seems satisfied with just the two and then he's sort of quiet for a little bit, acting like he wants to say something else.

"You know," he finally says, leaning up against my dresser, "I really *do* want you to be in this band. I know I said I didn't, but I do. It'll be fun for you and that's what matters. So, you know, don't worry about me. Just go ahead and be in the band. Okay?"

"Thanks, Dad," I say, sitting there in my pajamas, hugging the bass against my chest, "but it's too late. The guy starting that band picked someone else. He called on Friday. He didn't want me."

Dad looks genuinely sorry to hear this. "Is that why you've been up here all weekend?"

I sort of want to say, *Yeah, plus the fact that you're a drunk and I hate you*, but instead I just say, "Yeah, pretty much."

Dad stands there for awhile, looking down at the floor. Finally, he says, "I wish your mom was here. She was so much better with this sort of thing. With everything, really." He looks at the floor some more, rocking back and forth a little, and I wonder if maybe he's done, but then he says, "She started a band. Did you know that? Started the whole thing. Actually, she started a couple bands." He looks up at me. "Think you could you do that? Start a band?"

"Me? No. I'm not good enough."

"Neither was she. Not when she first started."

And then he tells me about how Mom was in a band when they first met, back in college. How they weren't anything special, but it was cool anyway and something fun to do when she was sick of studying. He tells me about how they played a few parties and how cool that was. How cool *she* was. Then he tells me about the band she put together after graduation. Another band just for fun. Nothing too serious.

Standing in my doorway, telling these stories, Dad's got a smile on his face, looking happier than he has in a long time. I sit there on my bed, loving every second of it, wishing I could have this dad all the time.

"She put together a band in high school, too," he says, "but that was before I knew her. And that was a *really* simple band, because she was still learning how to play. She told me some of the songs they played. It was kind of like the stuff you just played for me. Simple stuff. You could do that, couldn't you? Be in that kind of band?"

Could I? I'd never really thought about it before. It seems a little... big. More than I could handle, maybe.

"Was it fun?" Dad asks. "Playing with that guy the other night?"

"Yeah. It was awesome. It was the best time I've had in forever." I almost want to add, *and then you ruined the whole damn thing when I got home*, but I don't.

"So, start a band," he says.

My mind is trying to wrap itself around all this to the point I'm almost dizzy and I say, "I can't believe you're telling me to do this. Didn't you... You *hated* the idea of me playing."

"I was wrong," he says. "You know? I've thought about it a lot and I was just wrong. You might as well get used to it. I'm wrong a lot."

Sitting there, holding my bass, I wonder if I should forgive my dad and let things go back to normal, but I don't know if I'm ready for that just yet.

Still, the idea of starting a band... It's really intriguing.

"You think I could do it?" I say. "I don't know

how."

"You think your mom did? She was a kid, just like you."

"But... how?"

"Jeez, I don't know," he says. "You'll need musicians. You know any?"

And then I think about who was at the auditions. I know them, sort of. I could call John Knowlson. I know him. Or maybe that guy Josh. He told me he thought I was good. We'd need a drummer, of course. And a singer. Or maybe I could sing. Ooh, that would be cool. Could I do that?

And suddenly, all these thoughts are racing through my head and it actually seems like something I could do. It would get me out of my damn room, at least. For the first time all weekend, I actually feel hopeful.

"Thanks, Dad."

"Sure thing, baby." He starts to head out and I wonder briefly if I should talk to him about his drinking. This little talk we had here was nice and maybe it's thawed things between us a little, but I'm still mad at him for being a drunk. Should I say something?

But then it's too late. I wimp out and let him leave without saying anything. One thing at a time, I guess. I'll deal with this band thing and maybe that will make me feel better and give me the confidence to tell Dad he needs to quit drinking or something. And who knows? Maybe he'll quit on his own. He was awfully helpful here today with the band stuff. Maybe he's turned a corner.

So I spend the afternoon calling people and trying to make a band. I call John Knowlson and find out he can't do it because he actually made David Nelson's band. Him and Ty and that drummer Kieran who was so pissy and almost got in a fight with David. So then I call that guy Josh and he's totally excited by the idea and says one of his friends plays drums and he hangs up to call him, then calls me back and says, yep the drummer said he'd do it, so then we've got a friggin' *band.* Sure, we've never played and we barely know each other, but still, we're a band. Josh and I talk about what songs we could play and he lists a bunch of songs that he knows, which seems hard to believe, since he's really not that good, but still, who am I to question it? So I say we'll definitely have to try some of them and then we decide that all of us should meet up tomorrow before school to talk and maybe set up our first practice and then we hang up and it's done. I'm in a band. Formed it myself. Amazing.

Oh, sure, it's not *the* band. But it's *a* band. And that's better than nothing, right? And if I'm in a band, even if it's not very good, that might still make me a little bit cool. We'll be all punk rock and indie and David's band will be the big, hotshot band, but people will talk about us like we're the scrappy new underground band and maybe that makes us cooler and more punk rock or something, like maybe we're the next big thing.

And those are the daydreams running through my head as I finally get my lazy ass out of bed and into a shower and downstairs to eat some actual food and then guess who calls me? Audrey! She says she's over at Austin's house and David is having his first rehearsal and I am so lucky I didn't make his band because they are already fighting and it's a friggin' nightmare and she'll give me all the details tomorrow and then I'm about to explode with happiness because Audrey Gill is still my friend! I didn't make David's band, but she still likes me. Of course, maybe she has some psychic superpowers and was just waiting until I formed my own band before she called, but if she can read minds like that, then, really, who knows what else she can do, probably fly or turn invisible or something, but I'm just being silly now, but it doesn't matter because everything is wonderful and will be forever and ever.

And that feeling lasts for a few hours.

But then that night, Dad gets drunk again. *Really* drunk. And he puts on Mom's favorite movie and watches it with the volume blasting and so that's what I get to listen to while I'm trying to fall asleep.

Well, I guess I can't have everything. At least Dad and I made up a little. That's something, right? And he got me to form this band, so that's definitely something, right?

Okay, fine. He's still a drunk and I still hate it. I tell myself I'll deal with it later, but in truth, I'll just *not* deal with it because I'm a wimp and a loser.

But I'm in a band. And I've got a friend. A cool friend. And that ain't bad.

Chapter 12

The drummer's name is Luke and we're over at his house, playing in his garage.

Or, rather, we're *not* playing in his garage. I'm *wishing* we could play, but we can't quite seem to get there.

It all started with Josh picking me up at my house. I was waiting there by the door, because I really didn't want Josh to come inside. Sure, my dad's not going to be drunk at 11 o'clock on a Saturday morning, but still. So as soon as Josh's car pulls up out front, I'm out the door, bass in one hand, amp in the other. Mom's amp is crazy-heavy, by the way. It's got wheels on the bottom, but that doesn't help with stairs and getting it into Josh's car. Bass players must be stronger than other musicians, just from hauling all this stuff around.

So, I'm totally psyched to get started, but Josh wants to stop on the way to Luke's and get some coffee, and maybe that would be fine if he just got it to go, but no, he wants to sit down and drink it there, and this annoys the hell out of me, but I don't really feel like I can complain about it, because, honestly, I hardly know the guy and it's the first practice for our new band, and maybe this is just something that goes along with being in a band, I don't really know, do I? So I sit there in the coffee shop with Josh, bouncing my knees up and down, wishing he'd hurry up so we could get started with the whole *band* thing, you know, but he's in no hurry and wants to chat about school and stuff and I'm a wimp and put up with it and then *finally* he finishes his stupid coffee and we get back in the car and head to Luke's.

Except we don't head to Luke's. We go in the exact opposite direction, to this pawn shop where Josh wants to show me this guitar amp and I'm like, who cares about a stupid guitar amp, let's just go to Luke's already. But once again, I don't say this, because once again, I don't really know anything about bands and guitarists and how it's all done. So I sit there while Josh shows me the amp and then he asks the guy there if he can try it out and he uses one of the guitars that are for sale there and plays a song he knows which I don't know and he asks me what I think of the amp and I don't think anything about the amp, I just think we should leave already. But we don't. Josh just plays another couple songs and I'm going crazy wanting to leave and it seems like we've been there forever and then *finally* I grow a spine and tell Josh we should leave, so we do and, believe it or not, this time we actually go to Luke's.

So Luke's place is okay, I guess. I don't really know the guy. He's a junior, same as me, but I'm not sure I've ever had a class with him before, he's just this sort of generic-looking blond kid, nothing special. He's shorter than me, but who isn't? Anyway, we're at his house, which smells kind of funny, sort of like soup, but I guess probably everyone's house smells funny. God knows what mine smells like. Scotch, probably. But anyway, Luke seems fine, and I'm getting more and more excited, ready to start rocking out, but then we find out Luke's drums aren't in the garage, they're in his room, so he's got to take apart his whole kit and carry it to the garage and then put it together again and Josh and I help a little but there's only so much we can do and it all just seems to take forever. To be honest, I'm not sure Luke's ever done this before, taking apart his kit and then setting it up again, because he keeps putting pieces together wrong. Finally, though, he's got it all put together and I'm psyched but then Josh realizes that he forgot his guitar cord and I can't loan him mine because it's the only one I've got, so he's got to drive back to his house to get it. Well, I stay behind and fiddle around on my bass in the garage and I'd love to say that Luke and I had fun fiddling around together, but he doesn't even stick around, he just goes back in his house to watch TV and I'm like, what the fuck, so I'm out there in Luke's garage by myself, playing along with my iPod, and Josh takes *forever*, I swear to God it was like an hour and a half or something, he could've stopped and gotten lunch, it took so long. So I'm really friggin' annoyed by the time he comes back and just want to play already, so I send Josh into the house to get Luke and they finally come back out and then we're all there in the garage and we've all got everything we need and then, dear sweet Jesus, I didn't think it was possible, we actually *play*.

And it sucks.

We're playing "Wild Thing." Josh told me Luke knew it, but clearly he doesn't. "Wild Thing's" got all these pauses through it, where everyone sort of stops while the singer sings. Well, the first time through, Josh and I make those pauses, but Luke just keeps on playing. I'm singing, of course, but we don't have a microphone or an amp for the vocals, so I'm just trying to sing really loud. This would probably have worked a little, but if Luke just keeps on playing? You can barely hear me at all. And, trust me, I'm screaming.

When we get to the end, Josh is like, "That sounded pretty good!"

So, I'm thinking, what, are you kidding me? I don't

say this, of course, but I don't really know what to say. How should I handle this? It's my first band, how would I know? So I try to be diplomatic.

"Um, yeah, that had some good parts." I chew my lip for a second, then try, "So, let's give it another go. And this time, Luke, why don't you..." And I try to explain how the song goes.

I can't tell what he thinks of this – I just met the guy – but then we go through the song again and it's better. Actually, I barely sing this second time through. Mostly, I'm sort of coaching Luke through it. When we finish, we try it a third time and then a fourth and, to be honest, it's sounding better and better and is almost sort of fun by the end. I'm digging the noise and the volume and the way it punches you in the chest and all that, but I'm also sort of digging the way we're having to help each other through it. It's like Mr. Nelson said back at the auditions: if you look at the other musicians, it helps you play better. So I'm locking in on both Luke and Josh, trying to drag them through the song, and it's kind of of fun. We don't sound all that great – certainly not as good as things did at David Nelson's – but after four times through the song, it's halfway decent. Not a trainwreck, at least.

"Cool, guys," I say. "We're getting there. You wanna go through that again? Or should we try something new?"

From behind the drums, Luke says, "Actually, I've

gotta go. We're going to my uncle's."

At first, I think he must be joking. "What? We just started."

Luke holds up his phone for me to see. "Yeah, but it's four o'clock. I've gotta go."

Four o'clock? Josh picked me up at eleven. It's been five hours? And we've played for, what, thirty minutes? You've got to be kidding me.

Josh can tell I'm annoyed. "We can play again next week," he says.

"Um, actually," Luke says, "I'm gonna be gone next weekend."

I'm looking at the other two in amazement, but honestly don't know what to say. Finally, I just turn off my amp, unplug my bass, and start packing up.

Five hours. And all we played was four songs. Or rather, one song, four times. What a joke.

On the drive home, Josh is sort of apologetic. "I thought Luke was gonna be better than that."

"He didn't even know the song," I say.

"Yeah. But by the end, he sounded pretty good, didn't he?"

This is debatable, but I don't get into it. What I really want to do is start yelling about how we wasted four and a half hours doing *nothing*, but I guess I'm a wimp because I just sit there and stew while Josh drives me home.

Later that day, I get a call from Josh telling me that Luke doesn't want to be in the band anymore.

"One practice and he's done?" I say.

"He said he was too busy."

"Too busy doing what? Watching TV? He's certainly not too busy practicing his drumming. I thought he wanted to play with us."

"I thought he did, too," Josh says. "I guess he changed his mind or something."

So I'm in a funk the rest of the day. The whole weekend, really. But on Monday morning, on the bus ride to school, I sit with John Knowlson and tell him the whole story. He tells me about a couple guys he knows who play drums, including this kid Aaron who's in the school jazz band. So that day after lunch, Audrey and I go to the band room and watch the jazz band for a little and there's Aaron playing and he's actually pretty decent. Better than Luke, that's for sure. And when I call him that night, he seems like an okay guy.

"Yeah," he says, "I'll play with you guys. It'd be fun."

I decide I need to be a little brave, so I say, "Now, listen, don't just say that. Our last guy flaked out after one practice. Do you really want to be in a band?"

He says he does and I guess I have to believe him, so I tell him to work on "Wild Thing" and then I throw a couple other songs at him that maybe we could play and he says he'll learn them by Saturday and then it's set. We've got a drummer again. And this time, I picked him, not Josh, so it feels different. It feels like *my* band. Which is cool.

Chapter 13

"Why don't *you* play an instrument?" I say to Audrey. "I'd totally have you in my band."

"I played cello in middle school," she says. "You need a cello player? I wasn't very good. And I don't have a cello."

"I guess you could play air cello. We need one of those."

It's Thursday after school and Audrey and I are at the Bullfrog Cafe, drinking lattes and talking. Her friend Priscilla's here, too, but she doesn't seem all that interested in joining the conversation. She's mostly just looking out the front window and playing with her hair, which is super-straight and dyed jet black. Priscilla's one of the coolest-looking people at our school. Today she's wearing this tight black top and a plaid mini-skirt with black tights and a vintage black leather jacket over all of it. I wish I had her clothes. So punk rock.

"I want to come to your practice on Saturday," Audrey says. "Can I? I want to see if it's as bad as you say."

"I won't let it be that bad," I say. "That was just ridiculous."

Without even looking over at us, Priscilla says, "You won't be as good as David Nelson's band. I hear they're gonna *kick ass*."

There's a bit of silence then. Priscilla has a way of saying things that makes it seem like she's insulting you. I don't like it, but what can I do? She's Audrey's friend.

Fortunately, Audrey steps in. "Well, maybe," she says carefully.

"I hear they're fabulous," Priscilla says. "I hear David Nelson is amazing. The best musician at our school."

Audrey gives me a quick glance across the table. It seems like maybe Priscilla throws her off a little bit, too. "It's hard to tell so far. From what I've seen, at least."

Priscilla gives her a look and raises an eyebrow. "Oh, that's right. Your *boyfriend*." Then, slowly and gracefully, she rises from her seat like a panther and grabs her bag. "Well, anyway, I'm leaving. Things to do, people to see. Nothing either of you would be interested in." And then she leaves the cafe, the door tinkling behind her. I watch her through the front window, heading up the sidewalk. She walks like she's a queen. The queen of badasses. I wish I could walk like that.

Across the table from me, Audrey's staring into what's left of her latte. Her hair is dyed blue now. She just dyed it yesterday, so it's really bright and fresh. "Priscilla's such a bitch," she says quietly, not looking at me. "And she doesn't know about David's band, either. They're really not sounding all that great. And I *would* know. Unlike her."

I take a sip of latte, feeling sorry for Audrey. Looks like I'm not the only person who's drifting away from old friends. "What's wrong with them?"

She looks up as if she'd forgotten I was there. "Oh. The band? Um... well, they fight a lot. I guess that's their main problem."

"That's not surprising, based on what I saw at auditions."

"Yeah," she says, running her fingers through her hair. "David's kind of a pain in the ass. He's got anger issues. I don't know what that's about. It drives Austin crazy." She sits up straight then and says, "Let's get out of here. You want to go to Arleta's?"

"Sure. Why not?"

Arleta's is this vintage clothing store a couple blocks away. We bus our table and head out the door.

It's cold outside, but sunny and nice, and as we walk, Audrey tells me about how arrogant David Nelson is and how he fights with his drummer, Kieran, and how John Knowlson tries to make peace but Ty the bass player seems to egg them on or something and they really don't get a lot done.

"Do they sound good, though?"

"Sure, I guess so," she says. "When they're not fighting."

"I wish my band sounded good. We can't even play one friggin' song." I sigh deeply, looking down at the sidewalk.

Audrey puts her arm through mine and pulls me close against her side. "That was your *old* band, sweetie. You've got a new drummer now. You guys are gonna kick ass. Just wait."

I can't help but smile. It's not really her words that comfort me as much as the way we're walking, arm in arm, like we're best friends and have been forever. Did I feel like this with Becky and my old friends? I'm not sure I did.

Arleta's is a tiny little shop, but they've got all sorts of cool vintage clothing. I'd never been until Audrey and I started hanging out, but now it's my favorite shop in the world. I bought a great sweater there last week and a pair of nerdy horn-rimmed glasses with a neck chain. I tried those out at school and thought I looked pretty good. Kind of a nerdy hipster look. Not as cool as Audrey, but still, better than my normal look, which is... well, I don't really have a look, do I?

Like I said, Arleta's is tiny, so when we get there and open the door, we can see the entire shop and everyone in it, and who's standing there at one of the racks? Damian Shaw!

He turns toward the door, sees us, and a big smile breaks across his goofy, handsome face. I immediately start smiling and blushing and I kind of want to rush up and hug him but also want to turn around and run away. Audrey's still got her arm in mine and she pulls me even tighter because she knows all about my big crush on him, so there's nothing I can do but walk into the tiny little place and face him, scared out of my mind.

"Damian!" Audrey says, still dragging me with her.

"Hi, guys," Damian says to us, still smiling. It seems like he's only looking at me, but I'm probably imagining that. Wishful thinking, right? I can't stop blushing.

It's then, however, that we see Damian's not alone. Hidden on the other side of him, poking her head around, is a girl. And I realize it's *that* girl. *The* girl. Damian's girl.

My smile immediately disappears.

"Hey!" she says with a smile. "Who's this?"

Damian moves so we can see her better and says, "Oh, yeah, guys, this is Skyler! Well, you know her already, Audrey, but Skyler, this is Maggie. She's a friend of mine from school."

Skyler is blonde and short and cute and perky and I fuckin' *hate* her. I just met her two seconds ago and I already hate everything about her and want her to die.

"So what are you two doing here?" Audrey says with a smile, still holding my arm. I'm glaring at Skyler.

"Oh, we just had a few minutes to kill," Damian says. "We're going to a movie."

The three of them talk about some stuff for a while then, but I don't really hear too much of it because I'm all pissed off about Skyler. She's being all smiley and talking with Audrey and holding Damian's arm and she's short and thin and she's got wavy blond hair and she's everything I wish *I* was.

And then I realize she's talking to me.

"Huh? What?" So smooth.

"Damian told me he's trying to get you to play basketball," she says, all sweet and horrible.

"Oh, yeah. Um, I'm not really an athlete."

"Yeah, that's what he said. I'm on your side. I told him to leave you alone. So you're in a band?"

"Oh, well, um, sort of." Jesus, why can't I be all smooth and cute and smiley like her? I try and smile. I'm sure it's a grimace. "We've only met once," I say. "And we already lost our drummer. But I've got a new one. We'll see."

"That's so cool," she says, smiling and holding tight on Damian's arm. "I hope I get to hear you someday."

"Oh. Yeah. Well, maybe. Someday." Nice, Maggie. You are soooo cool, aren't you? God, I hate myself! She's so awesome and I'm such a dumbass. And Damian's right there, watching the whole thing. I've got no chance with him.

Fortunately, they've got to leave then so they can get to their stupid movie, so we say our goodbyes and Skyler's super sweet and Damian gives me a little squeeze on the shoulder, which is actually pretty awesome, his hand all big and strong, but still, by the time they walk out the door, I've lost all hope of ever going out with him. Seriously, I can't compete with that.

Audrey and I are silent for awhile, just standing there in the middle of all the racks of vintage clothes. Finally, Audrey says, "Well, that was interesting." I don't respond, I'm just looking at the door, so she says,

"You're not gonna cry, are you?"

"She was just so..."

"Nice?" she says.

"Yeah. And pretty and perky and short and... perfect."

"The bitch."

"Yeah."

Audrey gives me a little hug then and I'm so happy to have her as a friend. She's so much better than any of my old friends.

"If it makes you feel any better," she says, "Damian was looking at you an awful lot."

"Really?"

"Totally. The whole time, he was looking at you. I'm not sure if he ever looked at me."

"You're just saying that to make me feel better."

"I'm not," she says. "He likes you. I'm serious. He doesn't want a little dwarf like her. She's way too short for him. He wants *you*."

I don't really believe her, but it's still sweet, so I try to smile and then we poke through the clothing racks for a little bit, though to be honest, I'm not really seeing anything, I'm just thinking about Damian and his adorable little buzz cut and his handsome straight nose and his chocolate brown eyes and then I get disgusted with myself and turn to Audrey and say, "This is bullshit. I don't want to think about Damian Shaw anymore."

"Okay," she says seriously. "What do you want to do?"

"I want to get a boyfriend."

"Okay. Um... anyone in particular?"

"I don't care. Anyone."

So we stand there in Arleta's going through a bunch of names, trying to figure out who has boyfriend potential, who's single, who might say yes if I asked them on a date. I tell Audrey I want someone tall, which actually helps the whole process, since Audrey's boyfriend Austin is on the basketball team, so she knows all those guys and they're all pretty tall. We finally decide I should ask out this guy on the team named Diego. He's single, he's acceptable-looking, he's about the same height as me, maybe a little taller, and we've got a class together, so we already kind of know each other. Plus, Audrey seems to think he'd definitely say yes because he's just moved here from Miami, so he doesn't really know a lot of people yet, so that's cool.

And that's where we stand when we finally leave Arleta's. I'm going to talk to Diego at school tomorrow and we're going to go out on a date and I'm going to have a boyfriend and I'm totally going to forget Damian and how tall he is and how handsome and how cool and how he's completely unattainable because he's dating this perfect little elf girl who can die and burn in hell. So there.

Chapter 14

Okay, so it's a couple days later – Saturday – and I'm down in my basement with my bass and my amp and I'm plugged in and playing and it's loud and I'm nervous because it's almost noon so the guys should be showing up any minute for our second practice. Well, the second practice for me and Josh. The first practice for Aaron Johnson, our new drummer.

We're doing it at my house this time. That last practice at Luke's was such a disaster, I want to have control over this one. I don't want people wandering off to watch TV. I don't want people having to cut out early to go to their uncle's. I want to have a *practice*. A real practice. A practice where everyone wants to be there, where we bust through the songs over and over, getting them so they sound halfway decent, where we act like an actual *band*, not just a bunch of dopes.

Listen to me. I sound like I know something about this, don't I? Pathetic. I don't know anything about being in a band or what a *real* practice looks like. I'm doing all this for the first time and here I am, acting like I'm some sort of experienced musician, not some dopey high school chick who's been playing less than a month.

Well, whatever. Maybe if I act like I know something, it'll all sort of work out. Maybe I can fool everyone into doing it right. Whatever "right" means.

My dad's upstairs right now, watching some sports game, I think. We're on pretty good terms right now, by the way. Now that he knows about the whole music thing, I don't have to sneak around all the time, playing my bass quietly in my room, setting up practices on the sly. He's actually been pretty interested in all of it, to be honest, so that's been nice. It's nice having something safe to talk about with him. Something that won't make him sad, won't make him want to get drunk.

He gets drunk anyway, of course, but at least I know it's not because of something I've done. And at least we've got that hour or two right after he gets home from work, when he's still sober and pleasant and responsible and my good ol' dad that I love and used to have all the time.

So I'm downstairs playing and then the door at the top of the stairs opens and I see someone's feet start walking down and they're carrying an amp and then I see that it's Josh. Even better, right behind him, carrying some drum stuff, is Aaron. Right on time. Imagine that.

Aaron Johnson's a sophomore and I don't really know him, but he seems like an okay guy. He's short and kind of athletic-looking and is probably mixed race because he's got green eyes and light brown skin and these short little hedgehog dreadlocks.

"Hey, Maggie," Josh says with a strange little smile. "I hear you've got a date tonight."

Well, *that* was unexpected. "How on Earth do you know that? Are you friends with Diego?"

"With that Mexican? God, no. But I hear things."

Now I'm even more confused, because, first of all, Josh hears things? He's got his finger on the pulse of social life in this town? Ridiculous. And, secondly, I'm pretty sure Diego's from Miami, not Mexico. And, third, there's just something about the way Josh said it that was ugly, like he was insulting Diego. Or me. Or the both of us.

Now, if I were cool or tough or whatever, I'd probably ask Josh if he's got some sort of problem or something, but I'm not, I'm just a big wimp, plus I'm all confused and off-balance right now, and anyway, I'm not even sure how I feel about my impending date with Diego.

Actually, check that. I do know how I feel. I'm completely unexcited. Diego seems like a nice enough guy, but I don't have even the tiniest crush on him. But what am I gonna do? I can't go out with the boy I want, so Diego will have to do.

And it'll be good for me, right? My first date. And maybe my first kiss. Though that's no sure thing. I'm not sure I'm the kind of girl who kisses on the first date. Am I? I have no idea. I wish Mom were here. She could tell me if I am or not.

"Okay, guys," I say, pulling myself out of that depressing line of thought. "Let's get set up and get started. I don't want a repeat of last week. Let's get moving."

So we spend the next fifteen minutes or so trooping out to Aaron's car and slowly bringing in all the drums and cymbals and cymbal stands and smaller drums and stands for those drums and a bunch of different sticks and these little pedal things and a little stool for him to sit on and God knows what else. Drummers have a lot of stuff. Way too much.

"Do you really need all this?" I ask Aaron as we're pulling the last of it out of his car.

"Well, yeah, I guess so." He looks like the thought has never crossed his mind. "It's my kit."

I'm not totally convinced he needs *all* of it, but then again, what do I know? I just know I'm sick of going up and down the stairs hauling all this crap.

After it's all finally inside, it takes another ten minutes for Aaron to put it all together. Faster than Luke, I'll admit, but still, this is annoying. There must be a better way.

Last week, in Luke's garage, we didn't have a microphone. I was just singing out loud and you couldn't hear it over the music. This week, Josh brought a microphone he borrowed from a friend, plus a mike stand and a cord. I suppose real bands have amplifiers that are only for the vocals, but we don't, so I just plug the mike into my bass amp. I have no idea if this will sound good.

I look at my phone and it's 12:30 and, miracle of miracles, it looks like we're actually ready to play. Can you believe it? Who says it takes four and a half hours to start a band practice? Not when Maggie Blackman's running things!

So we start off with "Wild Thing," of course, and it's not too bad. Josh and I have played it enough that it should sound good, and Aaron's really not that bad, either. We go through the song two more times and I see a few things that we can fix, like the way Josh is hitting the notes during the chorus, plus this weird thing Aaron's doing with his pedal-thing – he tells me it's called a "kick drum" – and so we fix those things and by the time we've done it maybe five times, it's really not too bad.

"Wow, guys," I say. "Nice job. I think we've got it." I'm a little sweaty but it's not gross and my face is flushed but I think a lot of that is just from being happy. I *really* dig playing music. A month ago, I'd barely touched a bass, and now look at me. I'm in love with it or something.

So we decide to start on one of those other songs I suggested, a Green Day song, and this one is a lot rougher, since it's the first time for all of us. Actually, we don't even really make it all the way through the first time, because I stop things so Josh and I can figure out the main riff. I'm pretty sure he's doing it wrong, so we get that sorted out. I think Aaron is pretty solid on it, but I can't be sure, this being our first time. Still, he sounds pretty good. Definitely better than Luke. Plus, he's smiling a lot and acting like he *wants* to be here, which is definitely a step up from Luke.

And so that's kind of how things go for the next couple hours. We work on those first two songs, plus this White Stripes song, and, yes, I know the White Stripes didn't have a bassist, but whatever, we play it anyway and it sounds pretty good. Since there's only the three songs, we kind of have to play them over and over, but maybe that's fine, since it's all pretty rough and we're just a bunch of beginners. Anyway, by the time two-thirty rolls around, I'm feeling pretty good about the whole thing. Aaron seems like a nice guy and he can play. And Josh is still pretty solid, nothing special, but solid. Best of all, we actually *played* this week, instead of wasting hours and hours doing nothing. I guess I can thank myself for that, since I was the one pushing everybody. So, all in all, I'd call it a success. Maybe this is what a band practice should feel like.

But, then, right as I'm feeling good about everything and proud of myself for making it all happen, it kind of goes to shit.

It's when we're taking apart Aaron's giant drum kit and hauling all the pieces up the stairs and out to his car and then trudging back downstairs to get more. At some point during all of that, my dad decides that he wants to quit watching his stupid game and start helping us. And I guess that would be kind of embarrassing for any kid, but for me, it's just mortifying, because Dad's *drunk.* Not crazy drunk or anything, but still, a little drunk. I can tell, that's for sure.

"Well, hey guys," he says to Josh and Aaron as we trudge past the living room. "How was the concert?" He's standing there and I can hear his voice is a little slurred and I pray the guys can't tell, but I certainly can.

"The practice was fine, Dad. How's your game? Shouldn't you be watching it? You don't want to miss anything."

He's all slurry and out of focus and says, "Halftime,"

and then, God help me, he starts following us downstairs. Well, I'm like, oh, please, somebody just kill me now, and I'm trying to convince him that we don't need any help but for some reason he really wants to help. He's talking too much and too loudly and I really don't know if the other two can tell he's drunk, but I can and just want to die.

At a certain point, as we're hauling yet more stuff up the stairs, Dad's foot catches on one of the steps and he almost falls. He's holding one of Aaron's cymbals and it hits the wall and makes this big metallic crash and Dad says, "Fuck! Sorry! I'm okay!," and I swear, I honestly want someone to kill me, right then and there. Fortunately, Aaron and Josh don't seem to be freaking out, so I tell myself that maybe they can't tell, maybe Dad just seems like a normal dad, only one who curses in front of kids. Then we finally get that load out to the car and I *finally* convince Dad that there's really only one or two more things left and he *really* should just get back to his game and so he does and Aaron and Josh and I finish up things and then they leave.

I let out a big breath, then go up to my room and flop down on my bed and look at the ceiling. I'm exhausted. I try to decide if today was a success or a disaster and finally figure it was somewhere in between. That's not too bad, I guess. Better than last Saturday, that's for sure. But I think that maybe I shouldn't have any more practices at my house, just so Dad won't embarrass me.

And then there's the whole matter of my date with Diego, which I should probably start getting ready for. I wish I could get more excited about it, but I can't. Still, I wanted a boyfriend, right? So now I'll get one, even if it's not *the* one. It's a start. Which, to be honest, is sort of like this band.

Chapter 15

So eventually I pull myself off my bed and into the shower, then start getting dressed for the date. The first date of my entire life. There are so many things I don't know. Whether I should dress up or not. Whether I should pay for everything, let Diego pay, or go dutch. Whether I should kiss him at the end of the night. And if I do kiss him, what *kind* of kiss? And it's not like I know a bunch of different kisses. I've never kissed a boy.

Jesus, I am so out of my depth here.

And so I'm trying on clothes and standing in front of the mirror, then changing into different clothes and messing with my hair and makeup and stuff and the whole time I'm thinking about my mom and what she would say if I could ask her for help. I think about her sitting on my bed while I change, giving me advice. I think she'd tell me to wear a skirt. I have no idea what she'd tell me to do with my stupid hair, not that I *can* do anything with it, it's so straight and fine. I wish I could ask her about the kissing. Was she a first-date-kisser? Or would she tell me to wait?

And would she tell me to quit talking to Damian Shaw in the hallways at school? Quit walking with him every day from Science to English? Or would she agree with Audrey that it's Damian who's doing all the flirting? That he likes *me* and not his perfect little elf girl, Skyler? God, I wish I could ask her what to do about all that.

I look at myself in the mirror, my hair in a ponytail, and I ask the biggest question. I ask it out loud to the empty room. "Mom, do you think I'm pretty?"

And then I have to fix my makeup, because I've started crying, and not just a little cry, either, but a big one, with sobs and tears streaming down my cheeks and, Jesus, I need to pull myself together because Diego's going to be here in just a little bit and I can't go out on my first date looking like this. So I breathe and dry my face and fix my makeup and I *don't* think about my mom or Damian or anything other than how much I like Diego and how I've got a big giant crush on him and how this is going to be the best date in the history of the world and if we kiss it's going to be amazing and he's going to tell everyone what a great kisser I am and eventually Damian's going to hear that and it'll make him want to go out with me.

And it takes a few minutes, but eventually, I'm cleaned up and ready to go. I've got a black skirt and that cool sweater from Arleta's and my hair's in a ponytail but with some loose strands coming down on either side and I've got on some makeup, but not too much, and some perfume, but not too much, and I go downstairs to wait by the door because I don't want Diego coming in. I haven't told Dad I'm going on a date. He just thinks I'm going to meet Audrey. The less he knows, the better. If he knew, he'd probably want to invite Diego inside for some kind of horrible man-to-man talk or something, completely embarrassing me. So when I see Diego pull into our driveway in his little gray car, I rush out to meet him.

Diego's already getting out of his car, but I sort of wave him back and he looks confused for a second but I just go to the passenger-side door and start to open it but it's locked and I look over my shoulder up at the house, worried that Dad might look out the window and see us, and Diego says, "Hi, Maggie. You look nice," and he says it in a way that makes it sound like he memorized the line ahead of time, which is fine, I guess, mostly I just want to get in his car and get the hell out of there, but the door's still locked, so I'm like, "Thanks. You look nice, too," and I'm still trying to open the door and I can tell Diego's trying to figure out whether to come around to open the door or to just get in his side and open it from there and everything's just as awkward as you can imagine, great start to the date, right? So finally Diego comes around the car to unlock it for me, but then he doesn't, instead he tries to hug me, which catches me totally off guard, of course, so I sort of flinch backwards at first, but then I realize what he's doing, so I come forward to let him hug me but we do it wrong and our foreheads knock into each other, kind of hard, too, but we try again and this time we hug but, as you can imagine, it's pretty weird, not natural at all, but then, *finally*, he unlocks my door, so I get in, and then he gets in, and we finally get out of there and start heading downtown and all I can think is, *Good lord, that must be the worst start to a first date ever.*

Things aren't a whole lot better in the car, really. Maybe a little. Like I said, I don't really know Diego all that well. He's just this guy who's in one of my classes. His last name's Alva and he's always seemed nice. He's decent-looking. Black hair, black eyes. Hair curly and a little long. Not super-great-looking, but not ugly, either. His nose is maybe a little too big.

"I've never been to this restaurant," he says as he drives. "Is it good?"

We're going to the Sycamore Gap Grill, which is downtown, across from the Bullfrog Cafe. "Yeah," I say. "It's good."

I'm kind of expecting him to say something after that, but he doesn't, and then we're driving in silence for awhile, but it's not a good silence. It's uncomfortable. So I say, "Have you been to the Woodstock?" That's the name of the movie theater we're going to.

"Oh, no," he says, "but my sister went. She liked it."

Diego has a little bit of a Spanish accent, and for some reason this makes me think of Josh calling him a Mexican. I kind of want to ask him if he knows Josh and if they're enemies or something but I'm not sure that's something I can ask, so I don't, but then we're just silent there in the car, driving along, feeling more and more uncomfortable, so I finally say, "You're from Miami, aren't you?"

"Yes."

"Is it nice down there?"

"Yes."

"Do you miss it?"

"Yes," he says. "Sometimes."

"I bet it doesn't get this cold down there."

This actually makes him laugh a little, which relaxes me. "No, definitely not," he says. "This is the first time I've seen snow."

This amazes me and makes me laugh and things get nicer then because we talk about snow and winter and stuff like that. It turns out that Diego's from Venezuela, but he's been in America since he was two. He says they moved up here from Miami because his dad got a job at the community college, and I ask if his dad's a teacher there, but he's not, he's something else, I'm not entirely sure what, something to do with supplies. It doesn't really matter, I'm just glad Diego and I are actually talking, so I can quit being so nervous.

The Sycamore Gap Grill's a pretty small place, but I've always liked it because half the place is an ice cream shop, so you can get sundaes for dessert if you want. We get a booth and a waitress comes and takes our order and the whole time I can't help thinking about how I, Maggie Blackman, am on a real live *date*. I'm not having dinner with my Dad or with a friend, but with a *boy*. It just makes it seem so much more important and I'm really aware of sitting up straight and having good manners and trying to make small talk and all the things I think you're supposed to do on a date. It feels sort of like work, to be perfectly honest, but still, I do it. I want this to go well.

And Diego's pretty good about it, too. He's not super-talkative, but we manage to have a conversation, and when the food comes, we both have good manners and we don't talk with our mouths full and, on the whole, I think things are going pretty well.

At the end of the meal we decide to go dutch but then the check comes and we're not sure how to split it up, so we decide that he'll pay for the meal and I'll pay for the movie and that seems like a decent way to do it. And, actually, to be honest, by the time we leave there and start walking down the street to the Woodstock Theater, I've decided that Diego's a pretty nice guy and I'm sort of glad I asked him out.

The Woodstock's a great movie theater because it's kind of old and there's just one screen and the tickets are really cheap because the movies aren't brand-new. If you want to see a movie as soon as it comes out, you go to the big Octoplex, way out on the other side of town, but the tickets are full price there. If you wait a couple months, you can see the same movie at the Woodstock for really cheap. Plus, they sometimes show old-timey movies, which is sort of fun.

So I pay for the tickets and then we get popcorn and drinks and I pay for that, too, but it's more than I'd expected and I'm actually a dollar short. I have to borrow a dollar from Diego, which makes me feel like an idiot, but he's cool about it, which is nice, so then we go in and find seats and wait for the movie to start.

Things are a little awkward in there, though. Maybe because it's pretty quiet and there's not a lot of people there and we're right next to each other, shoulders touching. There's music playing, though, so I think maybe we can talk about that, so I say, "Ooh, I like this song," even though I'm really pretty indifferent to it, but whatever, it gives me something to say. "Do you like music?"

He nods and says, "Yes," and then nothing else, which is kind of annoying, because I was hoping for a little more, so I try again.

"What kind of music do you like?"

He thinks about this for a little and kind of bobs his head up and down and says, "All kinds of music," and then he's quiet and that *really* bugs me because, honestly, what do I have to do, answer the questions for him?

So we're sitting there in silence again and it's back to being awkward and uncomfortable, but then the lights dim and the movie starts and so I can finally exhale and relax for awhile, thank God.

The movie's fine, nothing special, but when it ends, I say, "That was really good," just because I think that's what I should say. Diego says pretty much the same thing and, for the first time that night, it occurs to me that maybe he's as nervous as I am and maybe he's not sure how to do this, either. So I'm thinking about that as we leave the theater, and it makes me a little more sympathetic towards him, like maybe we're sort of in this together.

On the way home, we talk about the movie and things are pretty good and I'm thinking that this has been a pretty good date, on the whole, and then Diego turns his car into my neighborhood and that's when I realize, *Oh, crap! This date's not over! There's one thing left!* And I immediately forget all about talking and go into full panic mode, wondering if he's going to try to kiss me.

Time seems to slow down then and it feels like we're crawling past every house in my neighborhood and I'm wondering if he'll kiss me or not and whether I *want* him to kiss me or not and if he does kiss me, what kind of kiss will it be, and if he *doesn't* kiss me, how will I feel about that, and maybe I *should* kiss him, because, let's face it, I'm sixteen and I really should have kissed a boy by now, but honestly, do I want Diego to be my first kiss, no, of course I don't, but I can't kiss Damian, can I, and we're getting closer and closer to my house and I am *freaking out* by this point and then we pull into my driveway and I want to open the car door and run screaming up to my front door, but I don't, I just sit there paralyzed while Diego turns off his car, and then I'm like, oh, God, now I've *really* messed up, because the car's off and we're just sitting there in the car and there's really only one time a boy and a girl ever just sit in a car, it's when they want to make out, that's when it is, and we've probably only been sitting there for like two or three seconds but it feels more like half an hour and so I panic and say, "Well, I guess I'll go," and I try to open my door but it's locked and I try it again and it's still locked and so I completely freak out then and push my shoulder really hard against the door, trying to open it, and I say, "Why won't it open?" and then Diego unlocks it and so I open it but I was still sort of pushing against it with my shoulder so when it finally opens I actually *fall out of the car*, I swear to God, and so I'm lying there in the driveway, half in and half out of Diego's car and he's like, "Are you okay?" and I'm completely embarrassed, as you might imagine, just mortified, but on the other hand, I'm not sure I care because at least I'm *free*, I'm out of the car and away from any possible kisses and so I clamber to my feet and slam the car door and I feel a lot better, but then I realize I slammed the door right in Diego's face, so I open it back again and say, "Um, thanks a lot, Diego, that was fun, I'll see you at school," and he's like, "Okay, Maggie," and then I close the door, making sure not to slam it, and I rush up to my front door and I don't even turn around to see what's happening behind me, I just open it and rush inside and close it and I stand there in the entryway, my back against the door, and I want to die because, honestly, I just *fell out of the car*, right there in front of God and everybody, but, oh well, what can you do, and then slowly my panic goes away and my face cools down and I breathe in and out and make myself relax and I think, *I did it. I went on a date and I survived.*

Chapter 16

Okay, so it's Monday after school, and Audrey and I are in the school's gym, sitting shoulder-to-shoulder on these hard wooden bleachers, pressed in tight with hundreds of other kids, watching a basketball game.

Yeah, I know... Me? At a basketball game? Ridiculous.

But here I am, because North Sycamore High's playing their arch-rivals, South Sycamore High. And apparently we hate South Sycamore or something, because it's the only game all year that *everybody* goes to. Personally, I find the whole things slightly idiotic. I mean, why should we hate them? We're from the same town. Shouldn't we hate schools from *other* towns? It seems like the closer a school is, the more we should *like* them, not hate them. Because they're our neighbors, you know? But, no, apparently in sports it's the exact opposite. Your biggest rival is the school just across town. So when South Sycamore comes to play, everybody packs the gym and sits shoulder-to-shoulder on the hard wooden bleachers, cheering and booing and talking about how awful the other school is and how their students are so stupid and trashy and have poor personal hygiene and can't even dress themselves properly. What a bunch of nonsense.

The real reason we're here is so Audrey can watch her boyfriend Austin play and so I can watch my crush Damian play. And, yes, Diego Alva's on the team, too, but he doesn't really play much and, anyway, he's *not* my boyfriend, he's just this guy I went out with on a date.

"Okay, *that's* the line I was talking about," Audrey says, pointing down at the court. "Where DeAndre just shot from. What is that?"

"That's the three-point line," I say, trying not to laugh at her. "You get three points when you shoot from there."

"And how much do you get for a regular shot?"

This time, I can't suppress my laughter. "Audrey! It's basketball! You get two points."

"Well, excuuuuuuuse me. Not everybody knows these things, you know."

"But you come to games all the time. How could you not know that?"

"I don't watch the stupid game! I'm just here for Austin. To be a... supportive girlfriend or something. I thought you didn't like basketball."

"I don't. But my dad watches it all the time. He used to play."

"Couldn't help learning stuff along the way?"

"Something like that."

Down on the court, Damian stands up off the bench and gets ready to go back in the game, so I immediately perk up and pay attention. God, he's cute. I used to think David Nelson was so hot and, okay, yeah, I guess he still is, there's really no denying it, but now that I've gotten to know the two of them, gotten to know their personalities a little, Damian just gets better and better looking, while David just seems arrogant and volatile.

Audrey's been teasing me all game. "You know," she says, "your *boyfriend's* down there, too. You could be looking at him, instead of Damian."

"Diego's not my boyfriend." This is probably the third or fourth time I've said this today, which I'm a little ashamed of. After a moment, I ask, "Do you really think I should go out with him again? Were you serious about that?"

"Totally," she says. "You can't tell anything from

just one date."

I believe her, of course. Looking down at the court, seeing Diego sitting all lonesome at the end of the bench, I decide I'll call him that night. Hopefully he's not too mad at me for racing off at the end of our date like I did.

"Wait," I say to Audrey. "Would that mean I'd have to kiss him? Does a second date mean you *have* to kiss?"

"Oh, look who's full of questions. The same girl who made fun of me for the whole three-point thing."

"Seriously. Do I have to kiss him?"

"Of course not. You never *have* to kiss him. You never *have* to do anything. But why not? You've never kissed a boy--"

"Shhh!" We're surrounded by people and I'd rather not tell the whole school what a loser I am.

More quietly, Audrey says, "You've never kissed a boy. Wouldn't you like to? Just to say you've done it? To find out what it's like?"

She's right, of course. I would like to find out. I just wish I could do it with someone I was a little more attracted to. Like... oh, I don't know... Damian Shaw?

The gym's buzzer goes off and it's halftime. North Sycamore's up by three, for what that's worth, not that

Audrey or I care. We get up from our seats and start toward the lobby, where maybe we'll get some popcorn or something. Of course, every other kid at school has the same idea. It's so crowded we can barely move, but we slowly make our way.

Because I'm so tall, I can see over people's heads a little, and a little ways away I see David Nelson and John Knowlson walking together, looking like they're joking about something.

I tell Audrey and she says, "Yeah, those two get along great. It's the rest of the band that hates David."

"They hate him?" I say. "I didn't know it was that bad."

"Well, he's kind of a dick to them."

We slowly follow the crowds toward the lobby. "Do they sound good?" I ask, eager to compare them to my band.

"Yeah, I guess so. But I've got to be honest, Maggie, I try to avoid their practices anymore. It's not very pleasant."

I ponder this information as we shuffle out of the gym. My band's not that good musically, but we don't really hate each other. So that's something.

"Come with me to the girl's room," Audrey says.

"I don't have to pee."

"Then just talk to me," she says. "Priscilla's here and I don't want to run into her."

When Audrey and I first started hanging out, I thought she was the coolest of the cool. A super-person, basically. Now that we're closer, I know that she's got her problems, her insecurities, just like me. She's even got old friends she'd like to avoid, so I guess I can help her with that.

We settle in at the back of the line for the girls room, probably twenty girls in front of us. Looking over the crowd, I spot Priscilla across the lobby. She's with another one of Audrey's old friends, buying drinks. I tell Audrey and she immediately bends over and pretends to tie her shoelaces. "Tell me when she's gone," she says.

I move so Audrey can hide behind my legs. "Did you two get in a fight?"

"No," she says, still bent over. "I'm just sick of her. I used to like her, I guess. Actually, I don't know if I ever did. She's kind of a bitch, you know?"

Yeah, I definitely know that. Priscilla's stylish and exciting and cool, but she isn't actually nice.

My thoughts are interrupted by someone saying, "Hey."

I look up and it's Becky, my old friend, who I haven't spoken to in... jeez, it seems like weeks. Behind her are Ginger and Patty. All three of them are smirking, arms crossed, eyes narrowed.

"Oh, hi, guys," I say, trying to smile. I can feel myself blushing. These used to be my best friends. Now they just look like strangers. Unfriendly strangers. "How's it going?"

"Good," Becky says, still smirking. "But the three of us were just wondering; are you still doing that stupid music thing?"

"Um, yeah. The band, you mean?"

Ginger giggles and Patty says, "If you want to call it a band." Ginger giggles more.

I feel like I've just been slapped. What's going on here? We used to be friends.

"No, it's not a band," Becky says, arms folded across her chest, looking as mean as I've ever seen her. "David Nelson's in a *band.* What you're doing, that's just a joke. Everybody says so."

"We all got invited to David Nelson's party this weekend," Patty says. "Did you? No? What a surprise. Well, I guess you'll just have to hang out with your *band.*"

Right then, Audrey stands up, no longer pretending to tie her shoes. She steps forward, getting right up in Becky's face. "Who the fuck are you?" Audrey says. "And what do you think you're doing, talking to my friend like that?"

Becky backs up, looking terrified. She stammers a few times, tries to regain her composure, then says weakly, "Well... who are *you*?"

"I'm Audrey Gill. And I'm friends with Maggie. And I swear to God I'm gonna piece you right in the fuckin' head if you give my friend any more shit." Audrey's no bigger than the other girls, but right now, she's definitely scarier. "So why don't you three sorority girls just shut your traps, and hike your boney little asses back to your croquet game or your poodles or whatever it is dried-up bitches like you do."

She stares at the three of them, silently daring them to do something, but all they do is scurry away, clustered together for safety.

After a moment of watching them disappear, Audrey turns back to me. She takes a deep breath, exhales, and says, "Well. That was unpleasant."

I'm staring at her, wide-eyed. "My. God. Audrey."

She looks sheepish and apologetic. "Yeah, I know. Sometimes I go to the angry place."

"I guess so."

"I don't like bullies."

"I guess not."

All the other girls in line start quietly talking again,

but it's clear they're talking about us and what Audrey just did. Looking across the lobby, I can see that Priscilla saw the whole thing, too.

Audrey and I just stand there in the middle of it all, everyone looking at us. I've never felt prouder to be friends with someone.

Chapter 17

"Maggie? Maggie?"

I shake my head. "Huh? What?"

Josh and Aaron are looking at me. We just finished playing a song.

"Anyone home?" Aaron says from behind his drum kit, laughing.

"Sorry, guys." I've been doing that all day. Fading out, thinking about other stuff when I should be thinking about the music. "That sounded pretty good."

We're working on a White Stripes song. I have to admit, it's pretty impressive that I can play and sing a song all the way through while my mind wanders off, thinking about other stuff.

Okay, I guess I should 'fess up. I'm not thinking about "other stuff." I'm thinking about kissing. Specifically, kissing Diego last night, after our date.

I know. Crazy, right? I finally kissed a boy! It wasn't a boy I'm all that into and the date wasn't all that special, but nevertheless, I, Maggie Blackman, have now kissed a boy.

And it was great.

Seriously, it was *fabulous*. How have I gone this long without kissing? It's the best thing *ever*.

Okay, so here's how it happened.

It was Friday, right? And it was our second date. And, to be honest, it really wasn't that much better than the first date. I figured I should give Diego a second chance, just to see if things would improve, but, no, they didn't, really. We had dinner and then we kind of walked around awhile – we were downtown – and the conversation was kind of weak and I was never entirely comfortable and I don't think he was, either. On the whole, there was nothing to make me think there would be a third date.

But then we were walking in this park and it was a little cold, not too bad, and we ended up stopping on this bridge that goes over this creek. It was in kind of a quieter spot, so we stopped and were looking down at the water. Just looking, nothing special. It's quiet and nice.

And then Diego says, "You're so pretty."

Well, that was a shock. He hadn't said anything like that to me before. Still, it was cool, I guess. I mean, everyone likes to hear they're pretty, right?

So I say, "Thanks," and then I'm wondering if I should tell him he's handsome, just to be nice or something, but I'm not sure what the etiquette is on that sort of thing.

And so I'm wrestling with that in my mind when Diego says, "Can I kiss you?"

Well, that *really* throws me for a loop. My mind starts racing and I'm kind of freaking out a little, so it's not even the tiniest bit romantic. A first kiss is supposed to be *romantic*, right? But this one isn't, because I'm standing there on that bridge in a panic, wondering what the hell to do.

But I somehow manage to say, "Okay. Sure."

And so Diego leans in, and I lean in, and our noses kind of bump into each other, but then we tilt our heads like they do in the movies and everything's in slow-motion and I'm freaking out, but then we kiss.

And it's *fantastic*.

Seriously, it's so great.

I'm not sure why, but I always figured people started with normal kissing and then worked their way up to french kissing. But no, when Diego and I kissed, that tongue was right in my mouth and I know I probably should have been grossed out by it, but I wasn't. It was fantastic. It was a shock, of course, but it was also sensational. I remember thinking, *Wow, I could get used to this!* Isn't that awful? Well, whatever. I don't care. I kissed a boy. I *french* kissed a boy. And I liked it.

So now, here I am at band practice, and I can't keep my head straight because I'm thinking about the kiss, but Josh and Aaron are looking at me, and I figure, well I'm the leader of this band and everything, I really do need to focus, so I shake off all the kissing memories and try to get my head back into the music.

"Okay. Yeah. Alright." I'm bobbing my head up and down, trying to think. I grab my phone off the top of my amp and see we have about fifteen minutes left. "Okay, let's go through them all again," I say. "Just once through, back-to-back, then we'll call it a day."

So we do and it all sounds pretty good. For a bunch of newbies, at least. We're still not good enough to play the songs exactly how they're meant to be played, but we fake our way through.

A couple days ago, David Nelson's band played a lunchtime show at school. It was only three songs and it was just a small thing out in front of the cafeteria, but it was still pretty fantastic. They nailed those songs, note for note.

Us? No, we're not quite there yet. But we're getting better.

I read this thing on the internet saying you should record yourself as much as possible, so that's what I'm doing. My phone's got a little audio recorder, and I'm recording this last go-through. I'll listen to it later and maybe spot some things we can do better. That's the theory, at least.

We're at Josh's house, by the way, playing in his bedroom. It's a pretty big bedroom, I guess, but we're still kind of tight, what with the drum kit and the two amplifiers and the microphone stand and all that. It's better than being at my house, though, worried the whole time that Dad will embarrass me.

When we finish, we start packing up our stuff. We're getting better at dealing with all our equipment. I'm getting used to how heavy my stuff is. Aaron's getting faster putting together and pulling apart his giant drum kit, which isn't quite as giant, since I convinced him to leave a few things at home.

While he packs up his guitar, Josh says, "So, are you going off to see Diego? Have some tacos? Talk some Spanish?"

I don't know where the hell that came from, but even though I'm not all that crazy about Diego, it's still an annoying and offensive thing to say. I kind of give Josh a look, but don't do anything beyond that because I don't really feel like having a fight right then, plus I'm a big wimp. We keep packing things up, and only ten or fifteen minutes later I'm in my car and heading over to Audrey's.

Yeah, Audrey's. She invited me to dinner. It'll be the first time I've been to her house. She said she had "something important" to tell me. She was being all secretive about it, but whatever. I'm looking forward to seeing her house. I suppose I'll get to meet her parents. Audrey and I might go out afterward.

When I get there, I see that her place is kind of a townhouse in this big complex. There are a bunch of houses side-by-side in a big circle and in the center there's a swimming pool and a tennis court and a community clubhouse sort of thing. I'm a little jealous of Audrey, having a pool. Maybe I'll be able to come over this summer and swim. We can get tans and talk about boys. I wonder if I'll still be dating Diego.

So I ring the doorbell and there's instantly a dog barking, right on the other side of it, but then the door opens and there's this lady who I assume is Audrey's mom and she's smiling and laughing, bent over because she's got the dog by the collar and he's going nuts trying to get to me, but he's not barking anymore, he's just kind of spazzing out, his tail wagging, and he looks like he wants to jump on me and lick my face.

"Hi, Maggie," she says, still laughing about the dog. "Come on in. He won't bother you. He just loves people."

So I go in – I left my bass and stuff in the car, of course – and I let the dog smell my hand and his tail's going like crazy and whacking into this potted plant that's right there and the house smells nice, not like soup, the way Luke's did, but nice. So the lady lets the dog go and he immediately starts bumping around my legs, sniffing everything, his tail going. He doesn't jump up on me, which is nice, and the lady says, "That's a good boy, Blackie," and Blackie gives a bark, which is kind of loud in the little entryway, but he really seems totally sweet.

I kind of put my hand out to shake the lady's hand and say, "Mrs. Gill?"

She's kind of stocky and has short graying hair and a really genuine smile and she shakes my hand and says, "No, I'm not Audrey's mom. I'm Rebecca. Audrey's mom's in here." She leads me into the kitchen and the dog comes with us, of course, still super-excited that I'm there, and then there's Audrey's mom, and it's obvious she's her mom because she's got Audrey's eyes and maybe her nose a little, too, though she doesn't have blue hair down to her shoulders like Audrey does, instead it's sort of blond and short and she's chopping something there on the counter but smiles and puts it down and comes over and, much to my surprise, gives me a big hug.

"Hi, Maggie!" she says, all smiles. "It's so nice to

finally meet you. Audrey just goes on and on about you."

Well, this is a big surprise, of course, and I get a little flustered and maybe blush a little, but I say, "Thanks, Mrs. Gill. It's nice to meet you, too."

And she says, "No, just call me Ingrid. We're all on a first-name basis here. Why don't you have a seat, sweetie. Audrey's up in her room, I think. She'll be down in a second. Are you thirsty? Do you want something to drink?"

So I sit at this table there in the kitchen and Blackie puts his head in my lap and his tail's banging into all the chair legs and Rebecca goes somewhere and I can hear her yell, "Audrey! Maggie's here!" and then she's back and she and Mrs. Gill – who I'm not sure I can call Ingrid, even if she wants me to – are chatting me up, asking me all about myself, and it's sweet and I like both of them and Blackie's sweet, too, though he keeps nuzzling my hands like he wants me to scratch his ears or something, so I do.

It's not too long before Audrey comes down, and she looks a little different. Not her clothes or anything, she's still dressed all cool, but she just seems a little nervous or something, maybe because it's my first time at her house. I'm not used to seeing Audrey nervous, she's usually so confident and relaxed, but whatever, she's still Audrey, right? So she sits down there at the kitchen table and Blackie goes over and nuzzles her a little but then comes back to me, because I'm new, I guess, and Audrey's mom says, "You actually got here at just the right time, Maggie. This fish is ready to go into the oven and it'll only be a few minutes. Are you hungry? I hope you eat fish. I should have asked. Do you?"

I do eat fish – I eat everything, really – and so the ladies continue to ask me lots of questions and Rebecca sits right next to me and is super-nice and Audrey still seems a little off, but I guess that's understandable. I'd be nervous if she came to my house, too.

Wow, actually, I hadn't thought about that, but she's going to have to come over eventually, isn't she? I wonder if I should tell her my dad's an alcoholic. I really don't want to. That's an embarrassing thing to admit. For me, at least. Maybe some people don't mind having messed-up parents, but I do.

So before long, the fish is ready and Audrey's set places there at the kitchen table and Blackie is in everyone's way and Rebecca shoos him out of the kitchen but he comes back just a minute later and then the four of us are sitting down and eating this great meal. The fish is really good, and as we eat, the ladies sort of ease back on asking me all about myself but they're still really interested in me and Audrey and our friendship. Mrs. Gill mentions Audrey's boyfriend Austin and how nice he is and asks me if I have a boyfriend and I guess things get a tiny bit embarrassing, since I'm not sure if I have a boyfriend or not, but it's not too bad because they're sweet and understanding and the food's good and, to be honest, it's been awhile since I've had a really nice family dinner. I sort of drift off then, thinking about my mom, but I stop myself, because I don't want to get all choked up and teary, and I do a pretty good job of that, and then the meal's over and Audrey and I clean up, then go up to her room.

"So, what do you think?" Audrey says.

I look around Audrey's room real quick and say, "Oh, it's cool." And it is, though that's not surprising, since Audrey's got such good taste. There are posters of bands and black and white photos and there's a guitar in the corner, which is odd, since Audrey doesn't play guitar, but whatever, I like the room and tell Audrey so.

And she's like, "No, not the room. Downstairs. What did you think of all that?"

I sit down in this old chair she's got in the corner and tell her the meal was great and her mom was really nice and so was Rebecca and so on, but Audrey still looks weird, like I'm not quite answering her the way she wants me to, but I don't know what more she wants, so I finally say, "Is that what you meant?"

She's sitting on her bed, not meeting my eyes, looking all mopey and nervous, which is not like her at all, so I'm going through my head, wondering what I've missed, and then it hits me. "Your dad! I just realized.

He's not here."

Audrey smiles and gives sort of a funny shrug and says, "No. They divorced a long time ago. Dad lives in Colorado now. I hardly ever see him. It's no big deal."

She still looks kind of unhappy about something, so I say, "Then what's the matter?"

It takes her awhile, but eventually she says, "Remember when I said I had something important to tell you? Well, that was it."

"Your dad?"

"No. What you saw downstairs. All of that."

I'm completely confused now and have no idea what she's talking about, but she's clearly miserable and wants me to figure it out, so I say, "Audrey, I'm so sorry, but I don't know what you mean. What did I see downstairs?"

She won't look at me, she's just looking down at her fidgety hands, and after a long pause, she says, "My mom. And Rebecca."

I have no idea what she's going on about and I'm about to say so, when it suddenly hits me. And I finally understand. I sit bolt upright with the sudden realization. "Your mom's gay."

Still not looking at me, Audrey nods her head.

Wow. Well, I didn't see *that* coming. Though, to be

honest, I should have. I mean, the whole scene downstairs, now that I think about it, it makes perfect sense. I guess I'd assumed Rebecca was some neighbor who just stopped by for dinner or something, but that's not at all how she acted. She acted like she lives here. Like she's part of the family. She acted like Audrey's mom. Or *one* of Audrey's moms, I guess. Yeah, looking back on it, it's totally obvious.

Audrey says, "Are you grossed out?"

"Of course not. Why would I be? I couldn't care less."

And so I go over to Audrey on her bed and I give her a little hug and she hugs me back and has a little cry, but it's not a sad cry, it's a happy cry, and then we sit there and talk about it a little and she tells me I'm the first friend she's told and then I buck up my courage and tell her about my family and how messed up it is and she's really sweet about it. I tell her I think I win the messed up family contest, because I'd trade with her in a heartbeat. And then we hang out in her room talking and listening to music and lose all interest in going out. Instead we go downstairs to make popcorn and Audrey's moms are getting ready to watch a movie and so we all watch it together and I end up leaving late but both her moms – I don't know whether to call them that. I'll have to ask Audrey – but both her moms adore me and tell me to come back anytime I want and I tell them I will. When I get home, Dad's asleep, thank God, so I just take a quick shower and get in bed. Audrey told me she'd come by tomorrow so she could meet my dad and I told her to come early, so she'd get him at his best, and so that's what I have to look forward to as I fall asleep. Not time with my dad, but time with my friend Audrey.

My best friend.

The best friend I've ever had.

Chapter 18

So the next few weeks are fine.

Dad's the same, I guess. Christmas was a little tough. It was our first Christmas without Mom, so, yeah, no surprise we had some tough times with that. But I can't say it was just Dad who was bummin'. We had a week off from school and I was pretty much a mess for all of it. The smell of the tree, the feel of the wrapping paper, all of it reminded me of Mom. Some stupid Christmas commercial would come on TV and I'd start crying. Awful.

So clearly, Dad's not the only one with problems. He's just the only one solving them by getting drunk. Which sucks.

He's still got moments where he's my old dad, of

course. Sober and cheerful and fun. I still love him then. But as soon as I can tell he's getting a little buzzed – and, trust me, I've gotten really good at telling – I make myself scarce. I disappear into my room, play my bass, learn some songs, do my homework, call Audrey. I've learned to adjust. Do I wish I had my old dad back? Of course. But he's gone now. And life goes on.

The band's still playing once a week and I guess we're sounding better. I'm finding Josh less and less pleasant, but so far we've survived. No giant blowups.

We're learning a new song every week. Not learning them perfectly, of course – we're still a bunch of rookies – but learning them enough to fake our way through.

I'm still acting as the band's leader and, to be honest, I like that. Partially because, well, who would have ever imagined it? A few months ago I was just this dopey girl who'd barely touched her mom's bass. Now I've started a band? And I'm giving orders? Keeping everyone focused? Crazy.

But I also like it because the band's one of the few things in my life I can actually control. Everything else in life just seems to happen to me, whether I like it or not.

Like Diego, for example. I have no idea what's going to happen with that. We're still going out, of course, but how do I feel about it? I honestly don't know. We have dates, we go to restaurants, we make out. I guess all of that's cool. I mean, I wanted a boyfriend, right? Now I've got one.

I guess I just thought I'd be head-over-heels for him. I thought that's what having a boyfriend meant. It meant the two of you were crazy in love. But that's not the reality. From what I can tell, having a boyfriend means going out to eat a couple times a week, going for walks, boring telephone conversations every night, and acting like you care.

God, that's so cynical, isn't it?

I guess it's not a complete disaster. Like I said, we've been making out, and that's a lot of fun. We usually do it in the car or on a park bench or, I don't know, wherever. Anywhere we get a chance, really. And when I say we "do it," I don't mean we *do it* do it. We haven't gone *that* far. Mostly it's just a bunch of kissing. Our hands kind of roam a little, which is nice. I guess maybe we've gone to second base, though I'm not actually sure what qualifies as second base. Does that have to be *under* the clothes? Because if so, then no, we haven't made it to second. But we're close. And it's fun.

I actually don't have any regrets about that side of things. I've learned how to kiss, I've done the whole feel-each-other-up thing. Maybe we'll go further, maybe we won't, but I'm glad we're doing it. I feel *smarter* somehow. I know things now I didn't know before dating Diego. So that's nice.

But does that mean I'm crazy about Diego? No. Am I happy to be dating him? Um... maybe? It's sort of okay, but it's also sort of annoying. I just wish I was more enthusiastic about the whole thing. I wish I *wanted* to spend time with him.

I wish I felt about Diego the way I feel right now, standing next to my locker, excited as can be, waiting for Damian Shaw to come walking down the hall.

It's become our daily routine. I get out of Science, grab my stuff for English, then Damian comes by and walks with me to class. It's my absolute favorite part of the day.

"Hey, good lookin'," he says as he walks up. He does that now and then. I know he's just being silly, but I still love it. "Goin' my way?"

"That depends," I say. "Are you going to Awesome Town? Because that's where I'm going."

He laughs and says, "No, I'm going to Dorkville."

"Oh. Well. Hmm." I sniff and arch my eyebrows, trying to look stuck up. "Well, I suppose I can walk with you for just a little while. But don't walk too close."

"Don't want to get any Dorky on you?"

"Exactly. And you look pretty contagious."

He throws an arm over my shoulder and pulls me close and I shriek and pretend to be freaking out and trying to get loose, but I'm not. I'm in heaven. I love walking with Damian. Chatting, flirting, just being together. Like I said, it's the best part of my day.

"So what's your deal?" he says as we walk, his arm, sadly, no longer around me. "You coming to the party or not?"

Oh, yeah. I'd forgotten about the party. Damian's *girlfriend's* having a party this weekend and he's invited me. "Erm... well..."

"You're not, are you?" He slouches a little. "Come on, man. I need someone to hang out with."

"Nobody's going?"

"Nobody cool," he says. "Just a bunch of South Sycamore people. Come on, it'll be fun!"

"Hang out with Skyler. She's cool, right?"

He shrugs and says, "Yeah, I guess."

"What about Austin and DeAndre? Hang with them."

He reminds me his friends won't be there, they'll be doing blah blah blah, I'm not really listening anymore, I'm mostly thinking about all that stuff he just said. Dissecting every word of our conversation, just like I always do with Damian.

He wants to hang with me because "nobody cool" will be there. That means he thinks I'm cool, right? It does, I'm sure of it. But he doesn't think Skyler's cool. That's what the shrug meant. "She's cool, right?" Shrug. "Yeah, I guess." *What's up with that? He doesn't like her anymore? He likes me? No. He just thinks I'm cool. Like Austin or DeAndre. Dammit! I don't want to be cool. I don't want to be one of his pals. I want him to like me. I want him to think I'm hot. Does he?*

"So what are you doing that's so important?" he asks.

"I've... I've got a date."

He slouches then and looks pissy. "Oh. Yeah. Diego." He's silent the rest of the way down the hall. When we finally make it to my classroom, he says, "You should cancel your date and come to the party." Then he's off, disappearing down the crowded hallway.

Well, of course, my mind's racing now, trying to interpret all of that. I'm practically dizzy with it, but somehow make it over to my seat. Audrey's already there, seated, waiting for me.

"What's up with you?" she says. Her hair's purple now, for what it's worth.

"The usual. Damian."

"Oh. Well. Big surprise." Bored, she puts her nose back into her papers, finishing up her homework or something. She's been saying all along that Damian likes me, but I've never been willing to believe her. But if he keeps doing stuff like what he just did out in the hall... well, I don't know what to think.

Boys are confusing. Why can't they be easy?

Actually, *everything's* confusing. Damian, Diego, my dad, my band. I can't wait until I'm an adult, so I'll know how to do stuff. Now, I'm just flailing about, trying to figure things out as I go along. It sucks.

Chapter 19

Okay, so we're at Josh's house, practice is nearly done, and I've got my phone out, recording us as we blast through our songs. And, yes, I use the word "blasting" because, in all honesty, we're sounding pretty good. Good for a bunch of newbies, at least. Good compared to where we used to be. Josh is playing these big crunchy bar chords, I'm thumping away on the bass, no problems, singing the whole time, and Aaron's beating the hell out of his drums. I've been on Aaron, urging him to play a little more aggressively. He used to sound like a guy in a high school jazz band. Now he sounds all punk rock.

As we finish, I can't help but smile. No missteps, no starting and stopping, no getting lost halfway through the song. We're turning into an honest-to-God *band.*

Amazing.

"Okay, fellas," I say, turning off my phone's recorder, "I guess that's it for today. Nice work."

I'm pulling my bass from around my neck when Josh says, "Heading off to see your Mexican?"

Bending over, putting my bass into its case, I roll my eyes, take a calming breath, and say through gritted teeth, "He's Venezuelan, Josh. I've told you this."

"Whatever. They're all greasy wetbacks to me. Did he swim across the border or dig a tunnel?"

I'm not facing Josh – I'm down on one knee, closing my case, latching it tight – but I know very well the smug look he's got on his face right now. It's becoming harder and harder to ignore him when he's being like this – which is far too often. I've gotten good at swallowing my annoyance and letting it go, for the good of the band, but now, hearing him mouth off yet again, I think about Audrey and the day she got up in Becky's face, telling her to leave me alone. What would Audrey do right now?

Well, that isn't a hard question to answer. I gather some courage and stand.

"You know what, Josh? I think I'm just about sick of the way you talk about Diego. And I'd like it if you'd shut up."

There's a brief look of surprise on Josh's face, but

then he recovers and comes right back at me. “What, you like all these Mexicans showing up? Not speaking English?”

“First of all... *dickhead...* Diego does speak English. And secondly, he's Venezuelan, dumbass, I just said that. And thirdly, what is your problem?”

“I'll tell you my problem,” Josh says, not even the tiniest bit intimidated. “I don't like all these people showing up, can't even talk English. This is America! Speak English!”

“Jesus Christ, Josh. I can't stand you anymore. You've got enough hate in your heart to power a train. I'm sick of it.”

Josh starts yelling. “Is that what your Mexican says? Why don't you tell him to go back to his own fuckin' country?”

I hate this. I just want to grab my stuff and walk out, but I'm trying to channel the spirit of Audrey Gill and fight on.

“Who else do you hate, Josh? Do you hate gay people? You want them to leave, too? How about Jewish people? Or black people?”

“Don't you call me a racist!”

I've got my case in one hand, my amp in the other, and I stomp over to Josh's bedroom door and try to open it. I have to put my amp down to work the doorknob. "You know what, Josh?" I say. "I love playing music, but I don't want to play it with you anymore. I don't want to be *around* you anymore."

I finally open the bedroom door, but before walking out, I look over at Aaron, who's been silent this whole time. "Aaron, this band's over. But if you want to play with me again sometime, let me know." And then I leave.

As I drive home, my hands are practically trembling on the steering wheel. I hated that. I really don't like confrontation. Still, I'm glad I did it. Audrey would have done it. She'd be proud of me. I wonder if Damian would?

God, what's my problem? I just got done defending Diego – who's only my friggin' *boyfriend* – and here I am, wondering what *Damian* would think of it. Pathetic.

Okay, that's it. I am totally and completely going to forget Damian Shaw and focus all my love and affection on Diego Alva. I defended him, he's a nice guy, he's a good kisser, and I am going to be an *outstanding* girlfriend from here on. Simple as that.

I get home and Dad's sitting at the kitchen table, a bunch of papers in front of him. "Hey, baby," he says as I come in.

I've just hauled my heavy-ass bass and my heavy-ass amp out of the car and up the front steps, so I'm more than happy to put them down and sit across from Dad. I rest my head on the table, closing my eyes, and exhaling audibly. "Hi, Dad."

"You look like me when I get home from work," he says with a laugh. "Your band sounds that bad?"

"We're not a band anymore." Without sitting up or opening my eyes, I tell him the story. It's a little tricky, since I still haven't even told him I'm dating Diego, so I just describe him as "a friend of mine."

"There will be other bands," he finally says. "With better people."

I sit there for awhile, my cheek on the table, Dad with his papers, probably paying bills. He mutters now and then, sounding annoyed.

My mind is on the death of my band. I'd been feeling so good about it. I'd started it, I was leading it, I was proud of it. And now look. I went and blew it up. Like a complete dumbass. Sure, it was time to tell Josh to shut up. Sure, it was time to stand up for Diego. But did I really need to destroy the whole thing? Other bands have problems. They don't break up. You think Green Day never had fights? They've probably had a ton, but look, here they are, what, twenty years later, still going strong. Me? One fight and the band's over. Nice work, Maggie.

So that's what I'm doing, head down on the table, feeling like a failure, when Dad says, "Okay, sweetheart, I've got good news. I think you can go to Florida after all."

"Huh? What?"

"That field trip. Spring break. I think you can go now. I've been crunching the numbers and I think there's enough money to send you. Great, huh?"

I sit up and ponder this. The Florida trip. With the Spanish club. I'd forgotten all about it. Last fall it had seemed like the most important thing in the world.

Man, that was *forever* ago. Who was I back then?

"You know something, Dad? I'm really not sure I want to go anymore."

"You don't want to go? What do you mean you don't want to go? I thought you were crazy to go on that trip. I've been moving money around all day, trying to figure out how to send you. And now you don't want to go?"

"I, um, well... I'm not sure I do anymore. I mean, I'm just doing different stuff now. Hanging with different people. I mean, Audrey's not going, and she's basically my only friend anymore."

"What about those other girls? You had lots of friends. Who was it? Beth? Betty?"

"Becky. She hates me now."

"Oh. I'm sorry to hear that."

“It's okay. Audrey's a better friend anyway.”

“Yeah, she seems nice.”

“She's the best.”

So I sit there for awhile longer, not really saying much. Dad keeps messing with his bills, I just kind of stare off into space. It's nice having these times with him, when he's not drinking, when he's just my dad. We don't even need to talk. It's nice just to be there.

Eventually, though, I have to get ready for my date, so I head upstairs, shower, dress, all that stuff. It's funny to think how nervous I used to be before a date. Now, I'm just, like, whatever. Clothes, hair, makeup, out the door.

As I drive downtown to meet Diego, I promise myself that I'll be the perfect girlfriend. Sweet. Loving. Devoted. I have no interest in Damian. I only have eyes for Diego.

And that's all well and good, but when I meet Diego at this little place called Youngblood's, I find that this date is just like all the rest. I can try and pretend I'm crazy about Diego – and I swear I'm trying – but it's just not real. Diego's a pretty nice guy. He's pretty good-looking. He's pretty friendly. If I were to rate him on all these things, with 1 being lowest and 10 being highest, Diego would be a 5, all the way across the board. He's just extremely, incredibly, fantastically *okay*.

Sitting across the table from him, eating my cheeseburger, I try to get past all that. I try to find our conversation fun and interesting and effortless. As we leave Youngblood's and walk towards the park, bundled up against the cold, I try to see Diego as gorgeous and sexy. As we stop in front of Arleta's and I look at the clothes in their front window, I try to feel oh-so-happy to be Diego's girlfriend. And as we continue down the street, heading for the Woodstock Theater, I tell myself that it's *my* fault. That if I were a better person, I'd appreciate Diego more. I'd be thankful for what I've got.

"Is that your friend Audrey up there?" Diego says.

It's starting to get dark and we're still maybe a block away from the Woodstock, but the sidewalk's lit up and I can see a good number of people gathered in front of the theater, including one with purple hair.

As we get closer, we hear music and singing and, yes, that's definitely Audrey. Then finally I see that there are people making music and it's Audrey's boyfriend Austin.

"Maggie!" Audrey yells, racing up and hugging me. "Isn't this awesome?"

"What's going on?"

"What's it look like? These goofballs decided to play on the sidewalk. Can you believe it?"

Well, no, I'm not sure I can, but there they are, right there in front of the movie theater, making music. Austin, DeAndre, and this guy named Bill. They make for a funny scene, the three of them: Austin – skinny, freckly, white – strumming an acoustic guitar and singing. DeAndre – also tall and skinny, but black – shaking a tambourine and banging a drum with his foot on a kick pedal. And then Bill – who I don't know all that well, but he's short and stout like a barrel – who's got this little flute thing – I kind of want to call it a penny whistle – and he's probably the best-sounding of the bunch.

"Don't they sound great?" Audrey says, her breath steaming in the cold air.

"Yeah, they do, actually. Are they... Is that a Beyonce song?"

Audrey laughs and looks like she's having the best time. "Yeah, they've been playing all kinds of silly stuff. They did a Lady Gaga song. It's totally fun."

And she's right, it really is fun. Their musical skills aren't anything special, but they all just seem so happy and energetic, it can't help but rub off on everyone standing there. And there's a decent crowd, too, though I can tell most of them are just waiting to go into the movie.

Speaking of which...

I turn to Diego, "So, do you want to go in right

away, or should we listen to another song?"

I'm really hoping he'll say we can stay, but of course, he says, "Let's go on in. We don't want to miss the start."

I try to hide my disappointment as we go over and get our tickets. As we walk in, I look back and see Audrey laughing and dancing as the boys play Madonna's "Like a Virgin." She's so lucky.

We don't miss the movie's start. In truth, we're actually way too early, which annoys me, since I'd rather be outside with Audrey, but I don't let it show, since I've decided to be the perfect girlfriend. So Diego and I chat, just killing time until the lights go down, and I'm trying to be super-interested, like a good girlfriend, but it's work, chatting with Diego. It always is and I don't know why.

Eventually the movie starts and it's pretty good, I guess. Whatever. But I still want to be a good girlfriend, so as we leave our seats and head for the lobby, I put my arm through Diego's and ask him how he liked it and act super-interested in his thoughts, but mostly I'm just hoping that Austin and his friends are still outside playing. They're probably not. Stupid movie.

But when we leave the theater, it turns out they're still there, still playing. And there's Audrey, still with them. She's not dancing anymore, she's sitting on the sidewalk, her hands wrapped around a steaming cup of coffee or hot chocolate or something. She's bopping her head, still looking happy, though maybe a little tired. The boys are... well, I can't actually tell what song they're playing. It sounds sort of like a rap song or something, the way they're singing. I let go of Diego's arm and rush over to where Audrey is, squatting down next to her.

"You're still here!" I say.

"Yeah," she says. "Not for much longer, though. They've pretty much run out of songs. They're just making stuff up at this point."

Watching the boys closer, I can see that Audrey's right. Austin and DeAndre are both rapping, but it's clear they're making it up as they go along, what with all the pauses and stutters and laughter and stuff. Bill is still on the penny whistle, just kind of playing along, making stuff up, I guess. It's all silly and fun.

When they finally decide their made-up rap song is over, Austin sees me there kneeling next to Audrey and says hi. "Do you want to play something, Maggie?"

There are a few pedestrians standing there, watching the boys play, and now they're all looking at me, so I instantly start blushing, and say, "I, uh... I don't know how to play guitar."

"Then you can sing. Come on, we need you. We've run out of songs." And then, without waiting for me to answer, he turns to the people there and says, "Ladies and Gentlemen, please welcome a guest vocalist to the stage, the lovely and talented Maggie Blackman!"

And then the guys in the band are applauding and Audrey's applauding and all the people are applauding and my face goes up in flames and I want to run away, but Austin's reaching down with his stupid long arms and pulling me to my feet and then I'm in front of them and I just want to die, but he says under his breath, "So, what can we do? We could do 'Baby' again. Do you know the lyrics?"

"Justin Bieber?"

"Yeah. Do you know it? Of course you know it, everybody knows it." And without waiting for a response from me, he turns to the other guys and says, "We're doing 'Baby' again. Maggie knows it." And then they all start playing.

Well, I'm absolutely mortified, standing there in front of all these strangers, but the guys are playing and, well, it's embarrassing to admit it, but yes, I do know that song by heart. I mean, who doesn't? I've only heard it a million times.

And so the guys are playing and I'm thinking about running away but then Austin and DeAndre both sing, "Oh, whoa-o-o-o," you know, like it does at the beginning of that song. And then they do it again, of course, and when they do it the third time, well, I can't help it, I just sing along with them and then it's the first verse and I'm standing there on the sidewalk singing, "You know you love me – I know you care – Just shout whenever – And I'll be there," and it's so pathetic, me, singing Justin Bieber, but it's also so much fun. By the time we get to the chorus, I've got this huge smile on my face and the boys are singing along with me and even some of the people standing there are singing along and it's just so stupid and ridiculous and fun.

When we come to the end of the song, I'm almost disappointed, it was so fun, and the crowd is applauding and so are the guys in the band and I'm smiling and laughing and just euphoric, really, and then, you'll never believe it, but guess who rushes up out of nowhere and picks me up in a big, giant hug? Damian Friggin' Shaw! I swear to God!

"Maggie! That was awesome!" he says, lowering me to my feet. "You were fabulous!"

Well, as you can imagine, I don't know what to think, my head is just spinning and I'm looking up at Damian with this insanely gigantic smile and then I'm hugging him again and then I stop and say, "What are you doing here? You saw that?"

And he's smiling down at me, too, and he says, "Yeah, I saw it! You were great! Have you been here all night?"

"No, it was just that one song. Austin made me."

I sort of motion back towards Austin with one hand, or at least I try to, because that's when I realize Damian and I are holding each others hands. And we're standing super-super-close to each other, too. I mean, pressed right up against each other, almost like we're hugging or slow dancing or something. And clearly Damian realizes it at the same moment, because then we're both sort of stuttering and letting go of hands and stepping back and we're both really embarrassed.

Well, guess who comes up to us then? Skyler. Damian's girlfriend. She puts her arm through Damian's and says, “It's time to go, *sweetheart*,” and then pulls him away, giving me the dirtiest look you can imagine.

I'm just dumbstruck, of course, my head absolutely swimming. I'm standing there watching them walk away and I don't even know *what* I feel. Embarrassed and sad and humiliated and then I remember Diego and turn back to where he's standing and he's looking right at me with these cold, narrow eyes. He shakes his head a couple times, then turns his back on me and walks away.

Well, I don't know what to do. I mean, Jesus, just a second ago I was singing Justin Bieber, on top of the world, and now I don't know what the hell's going on. I start to walk after Diego, but he's way ahead of me, so I have to jog to catch up to him.

“Diego, wait! I'm sorry!”

He stops walking and turns and says, "Don't bother, Maggie. I know you want to be with Damian. I see the way you two look at each other. So just do it. I'm not stopping you. Go be with him." And then he turns and walks away.

I stand there for a few seconds watching him walk away and I'm in a daze and I turn around and look back toward the movie theater. Audrey and Austin and the band and all the pedestrians, they're all standing there, looking at me. All of them. They saw the whole thing.

I turn and look for Diego, but he's already long gone, so then I look back toward Audrey and then I'm just sort of moving in a slow circle, not sure what to look at. Finally I just sit down, right there on the sidewalk, in front of God and everybody. How I keep from crying, I have no idea, I just put my face in my hands and breathe. And then Audrey's there and she's sitting on the sidewalk, too, hugging me and telling me it's okay, nobody cares, it'll all be okay, and then I really do start crying.

When I woke up this morning I was in a rock band and I had a boyfriend and now I don't have either one.

And it's all my fault.

Chapter 20

So. My life is over.

Which is never fun.

But, as bad as that is, trust me, it's even worse when your best friend decides to leave town for a week.

Audrey was really sweet to me on Saturday night, after it happened, but then the next morning, she and her moms took off for some sort of weird vacation/retreat. I don't even know what it is, but Audrey's missing some school and I'm missing my best friend. My only friend, at this point.

On Sunday, I barely leave my room, big surprise. I just lie there, looking at the ceiling. I listen to sad music. I think about how once upon a time I was in a band. And had a boyfriend.

There's no school Monday – a teacher training day – so that's another lost day, hiding in my room, wondering why the world hates me.

Finally, there's school on Tuesday, which gets me out of the house, but that's a mixed blessing, since there's no Audrey and I really don't want to see anyone else. I'm sure everyone at school's heard what happened to me Saturday and they're all talking about it. I get off the bus and walk in the door, feeling their eyes on me. I'm wearing all black clothes. It matches my mood. I should dye my hair black, too. And black fingernail polish.

Up ahead, against a row of lockers, I see my old friend Becky, standing there with Ginger and Patty. They're looking at me with matching smirks. As I walk past them, Becky says, "Hi, Maggie! How's your *boyfriend*?" Ginger and Patty erupt in giggles. My face bursts into flames. I wish I could just go home now. Not come back until next week, when Audrey's home. Maybe not even then.

Nobody else calls me out that day, but I'm pretty sure I heard some whispering and giggling that was meant for me. I feel completely alone. No one there to defend me. No one to tell me it's okay. At lunch, I sit alone. I eat a few bites, then leave. I feel like the whole cafeteria's watching me as I walk away.

As bad as all that is, it's not even the worst part of the day. The worst part is after Science. I go to my locker and get my stuff for English, then wait there, hoping and praying Damian will come down the hall, just like he always does, and walk with me to English. I wait forever. I wait so long that I'm late to class, but he never shows. I sort of knew he wouldn't, but it's still heartbreaking. The best part of my day, gone forever.

I see a few other people, of course. I see Diego. He won't even look at me. Just walks past, his jaw clenched, his eyes narrowed.

I see Josh. He's willing to look at me, but it's with this pompous, arrogant expression – curled lip and raised eyebrow – like all that stuff I said to him Saturday was a joke. Like *I'm* a joke. Hard for me to argue, really.

I sort of see Aaron, from a distance. He's on the other side of the cafeteria, sitting with some of his friends. I don't know if he sees me. I wish I had the courage to go up to him, to ask if we're still going to play together, but I don't. I truly can't bear any more rejection.

So all that happens on the first day back at school. I finally get to head home and I'd love to tell you that things are better there, but they're not. For whatever reason, that night Dad gets crazy-drunk. Just a complete and total mess. He's playing Mom's favorite songs on the stereo. Watching her favorite movie. I'm upstairs in my room, trying to avoid it all, but he's got the volume cranked, so there's no escape. At a certain point, I can hear him open the sliding glass door and go out onto the deck, which is awesome, because then the neighbors get to enjoy our happy little family, too. I should go down and at least make him close the back door, but of course I don't. I just lie there on my bed thinking of all the ways my life has fallen apart. No mom, no dad, no band, no boyfriend, no Audrey, no Damian. It's almost like I'm back where I started.

I mean, seriously. Am I any better off than I was when this whole thing started? I'd gotten things half-way decent for awhile, but now it's all back to zero. Like all that good stuff never even happened.

And that's basically my week. Monday, crap. Tuesday, crap. Wednesday, Thursday, Friday, crap, crap, crap.

You'd expect the weekend to be better, right? Wrong. Because I don't have any friends. None. Audrey's still out of town with her moms and there's no one else. No one. Plus, I don't have a band to practice with or a boyfriend to go on a date with. I don't have anything.

Oh, I've got a drunk dad. Sorry, I forgot. I've got that.

So I spend the weekend in my room, listening to depressing music and thinking about how I'll be alone and miserable the rest of my life. Audrey and I text back and forth a little. She's sick of her trip, ready to come home. Sunday night, she's texting me from the road, saying how they'll be getting in super-late, and that's when I get a text from Aaron.

want 2 play nxt wknd?

Well, as you can imagine, I'm shocked, but also thrilled out of my head. I have to calm myself down before I answer. **just u?**

ya. no josh. hes a dick.

Oh, music to my ears! So we work it out that we'll play next Saturday and it's probably the first time I've felt halfway decent all week. Yeah, I know it'll just be bass and drums and that isn't much, but I still can't wait. One, I'm addicted to music. But two, it's just nice to know that someone out there still likes me. That someone had to make a choice, and he chose me.

So the next day – Monday – I'm at school, feeling a tiny bit better. Audrey's there, so I'm going out of my way to see her. Stopping by her locker every chance I get, going down hallways I don't normally go down, just so we can chat for a second or two. It's partially to make up for lost time, I guess, but I'm also trying to remind myself that I actually have a friend. And, okay, maybe I want other people to see it, too. So they'll see that I'm not a *complete* loser.

So, I've got a friend again. Just one friend, sure, but

trust me, after a week alone, one friend feels like a million.

Plus, I'm still sorta-maybe in a band. And I'm not even wearing all black. In fact, I think I'm looking pretty good today. I'm wearing this vintage white shirt and a striped preppy tie under this purple sweater-vest, all of which I got at Arleta's. Underneath it, I'm wearing this green skirt – not a mini-skirt, exactly, but short – with black tights, because it's cold. Not bad, right? Maybe I *should* dye my hair.

I think about possible hair colors as I dig books out of my locker. Definitely not black. Purple might be cool, though. Purple like my vest. Only lighter. Lilac. Do they have lilac hair coloring? Audrey would know. She's the hair-dyer. Maybe we can do it this weekend. God, it's good to have her back.

"Hey, good lookin'."

I practically bash my face into my locker, I'm so startled, but I turn and look and who's standing there but Damian Shaw.

Yeah, I know, right? Damian! I sort of want to throw myself into his arms and never let go, but he's looking nervous and I'm definitely nervous and it's clear neither of us are quite sure what to do.

"Hi, Damian."

"Hi."

"It's been awhile."

"Yeah." He's silent for a bit, bobbing his head and looking thoughtful. Finally, he says, "I'm not supposed to be talking to you."

"You're not?"

"No."

"Because of Skyler?"

"Yeah."

"But you're talking to me anyway."

"Yeah."

We stand there in the crowded hallway for a few seconds, not saying anything, but it's clear this is an important moment. Finally, Damian says, "So, should we go to class, then?"

Walking down the hall with him, we're not saying a word, but it's still pretty wonderful. Our arms brush against each other a few times and I'm sneaking peeks over at him and he's sneaking them at me and when we get to my classroom, he says, "It was really good to see you, Maggie."

"Yeah. You, too."

And then we're standing there outside my English classroom, neither of us saying anything, but, I don't know, it's somehow okay. I really want to hug him but I don't. I hold back.

Because his girlfriend told him he wasn't allowed to see me, but he did anyway.

And for right now, that's enough.

Chapter 21

Well, it's a few weeks later and things are okay, I guess. When you completely destroy your life the way I did, it's not gonna fix itself overnight. I wish it were like that, but it's not.

So, yes, Aaron and I have gotten together, and it's been fun, but that doesn't mean I'm in a band. It's just a drummer and a bassist goofing around a little.

And Audrey's back, so I've got a friend again. But just the one. I'm not suddenly Little Miss Popular, with tons of people wanting to hang out with me all the time. Just Audrey.

And Damian's talking to me again, but that doesn't mean he's dumped Skyler and told me he loves me or anything. We're just friends. Which is nice. And horrible.

And Dad has his good days, but that doesn't mean he's suddenly sober and happy and reliable. He just has some good days. And some bad.

So things aren't perfect. But they're a little better. And I'm slowly fixing the damage.

Like today, for example. After a couple weekends of me and Aaron dorking around, just the two of us, we've decided to try and find a new guitarist. We're holding real, live auditions, too, just like David Nelson did, way back in November.

These auditions aren't super-packed, though. We don't have a basement full of girls, giggling and flirting and trying to get noticed. It's just me and Aaron and four boys. No gigantic fancy-pants room, either, with a pool table and a bar. Just my dingy little basement. We'd been playing in Aaron's bedroom, but it's too small for anyone but us. I put a sign on the front door reading, **Band Tryouts – Walk Around House And Knock On Basement Door.** I told my dad he can't come downstairs, no matter what.

The four boys trying out to play guitar are sitting on the basement sofa, squeezed in side-by-side. They all look horribly young. I look at the kid on the far left, a freshman boy with a mohawk. I'm pretty sure the mohawk's fresh. Like, he-cut-it-earlier-that-afternoon fresh. "Your name's Tony?"

"Yeah," he says, standing up. "But for the band, I want to be called Sick Boy."

"Sick Boy?"

"Yeah. It's from a movie."

I look at him for a few seconds, not sure if he's serious. "Why do you want to be called Sick Boy?"

"Because it's all punk rock!" He's got a big smile on his face. I doubt he weighs 100 pounds.

I sigh. "Okay, Sick Boy. Let's play."

Just like David Nelson made everyone learn "Wild Thing," I've had all these jokers show up ready to play a couple songs – Green Day and Social D, for what it's worth – and so Sick Boy plugs in, Aaron counts us off, and we play.

Well, you're not going to believe this, but despite the brand-new mohawk and the punk rock name, Sick Boy sucks. He jumps around a lot and bangs his head, but it's all an act, trying to hide the fact that he can't actually play.

The next three kids? They go by their own names, but aren't any better than Sick Boy. And none are as good as Josh. Not that he was anything special.

Aaron and I are rolling our eyes at each other, but we manage to drag the four crappy guitarists through two songs each. As we're nearing the painful end, there's a quiet knock on the basement door. I open it and there's a blond girl standing there, looking all nervous and intimidated, a guitar case in her hand.

"Am I too late?" she says. I assume this girl's from my school, but I swear I've never seen her before. "My brother was going to drive me here but then he got a call from work and... well... Did I miss the tryouts?"

"No, we're not done," I say. "You can still play. What's your name?"

"Emily. I'm brand new. We just moved to town."

"Oh, okay. You go to North Sycamore?"

"Yeah, for a couple weeks now. I'm just a sophomore. I hope that's okay."

"Sure it is. These guys..." I sort of wave a hand in their direction but don't bother to finish. "Why don't you plug in? You ready to go?"

"Sure!" She gives a little laugh and a bounce and I sort of want to hate her on principle, since she's short and perky, and that always makes me jealous, but she's not super-pretty or anything, so maybe I can't hate her too much.

Once her guitar's out and she's plugged in, we roll into the Green Day song.

Now, it would be really awesome right now if I could tell you that Emily just blew us away, that she was head and shoulders better than all the dorky boys – especially Sick Boy and his fresh-cut mohawk – but in truth, she's only okay. She knows the songs, though, and her chords are fairly strong. Plus, she looks at me and Aaron while she plays and has a little smile on her face and, to be honest, is the first person all day who doesn't seem like a poseur and a dope. That right there puts her firmly in the lead.

We're going through the second song with her, just approaching the end, when the upstairs door opens. I'm immediately afraid it's my dad, but then I see the feet and realize it's Audrey, who I knew was coming by. She must have let herself in. But then I see more feet coming down the stairs behind her and realize she's brought her boyfriend, Austin. And then I see even *more* feet and I realize, oh dear God in heaven, she's brought Damian Shaw. Damian Freakin' Shaw! She brought him to my house! Unannounced! I could kill her.

Well, needless to say, I completely mess up the end of our last song and then Emily's asking me how she did and I'm talking to her but I'm not really thinking about what I'm saying, I'm looking over at Damian, who's *in my freakin' house*, and he's making goofy faces at me, trying to mess me up and of course it works, I'm a total mess, stuttering and tripping over my words like an idiot, and I've got all these stupid freshmen boys talking to me, plus Emily, who I really kind of liked, and they're all packing up their stuff and then Sick Boy's asking me something, but I can't hear a bit of it because now Damian's come over and is totally trying to mess me up, he's put his arm around me and is whispering in my ear, "Booger booger booger booger booger booger," and so I'm laughing and elbowing him off me and he goes and sits down and I just wish all these stupid guitarists would leave already, but of course they don't and then Audrey's next to me, whispering in my ear that "Damian wanted to come, he kept asking if he could come, he wouldn't shut up about it," and I just want to kill her, I'm not even sure why, but finally, *finally*, all the guitarists are gone and then Aaron says he has to run but he'll call me to talk about the guitarists and then he's gone and it's just me and Audrey and Austin and Damian in my basement.

Damian.

In my basement.

"So how were they?" Audrey says, all stretched out on the couch with Austin, her back on his chest, his arms around her.

"Who? The guitarists?" I'm having trouble concentrating with Damian in the room. "Oh, nothing special."

"Nobody good enough for the band?" Austin asks.

I sit at the end of the couch, down by Audrey's feet. She's wearing these really cool boots. Vintage, of course. "I don't know. Maybe that girl. She wasn't too bad."

"Two girls in a band," Austin says. "*Sexy!*"

Damian's in the easy chair on the other side of the room. I wish I could go sit with him. I wish I could lean back on his chest and he could wrap his arms around me. "Did you hear about David's band?" he says.

"How could she?" Audrey says. "It just happened." She turns to me. "They broke up."

"No!"

"Yes! This afternoon. I was over there hanging out with Austin and he's working on my car and I'm making him lunch – "

"She's so sweet," Austin says.

" – and David and them, they're in the basement practicing. Fighting, of course, no surprise there, but apparently it was a little worse today, because I hear doors slamming – "

"She made tacos," Austin says.

"They were awesome," Damian adds.

" – and then David and John are coming upstairs and David is all pissed off and John's talking him down, but I can tell something's worse this time, I'm not sure why – "

"I ate, like, five of them," Austin says.

"I ate six," Damian adds.

" – but anyway, long story short, they broke up."

"Wow," I say, sitting there by her feet, trying to ignore the boys. "Who would've predicted that?"

"Um... everyone?" Audrey says. "Seriously, sweetie, I'm surprised they lasted this long."

"How did they seem?" I ask her.

She just shrugs, but Austin says, "David wasn't throwing anything, for what that's worth."

I'm sitting there thinking about bands and guitarists and whether Audrey was serious about Damian bugging her to come over here, when Audrey says, "So, we should go."

Austin jumps up and starts clapping his hands like a dork. "Bowl-ing! Bowl-ing! Bowl-ing!"

Damian's up, too, laughing and pretending to bowl.

"Are you coming?" I say to him. "Are you *allowed* to come?"

I feel bad because this sort of kills his good mood and he slumps there next to me. "No."

"No, what?" I say. "No, you're not coming? Or no, you're not allowed to come?"

"Oh, I'm coming," he says. "But, no, I'm not

allowed to."

Audrey and Austin are standing there together, looking at us, and Austin sort of coughs and raises his eyebrows and Damian tells him to shut up.

"You need to – " Austin starts.

"Shut up," Damian says.

"Look, if you're – "

"Shut up," Damian says again. "I don't want to hear it."

We're all silent then and it's kind of uncomfortable and then Audrey says, "Well. Let's go bowling, then. Everybody ready?"

I quickly make sure all the band stuff's squared away, and then we all head up the stairs, and I'm thinking about how this day has taken a big, big turn. Before, it was just gonna be me and Audrey and Austin, doing a little bowling, no big deal. But now, with Damian coming along, it's a very big deal, isn't it? It's almost like a double date or something. So I can't go out looking like this. I should go up to my room and try to pretty myself up a little. Would they wait for me? Just for a few minutes? I can't decide.

So that's what I'm thinking about when the four of us get to the top of the stairs and come out into the little entryway there by the front door, and I've just about decided that I'm going to go upstairs and change, when–

"Well, hey, guys!"

No.

Dear God, no.

It's my dad.

And he's drunk.

"Boy, quite a crowd!" he says, standing there in the entryway, leaning against the wall, a half-empty scotch glass in his hand.

The four of us are frozen in place, looking at him. Audrey's met my dad plenty of times – she's even seen him a little tipsy – but the boys haven't. Damian hasn't. I want to die.

Dad's looking at us, all out of focus, a drunken smile on his face. "Well, hey, Eleanor... umm... Abigail? Abigail!"

"Audrey," she says. She looks over at me, clearly mortified and not sure what to do.

"Audrey!" Dad says, too loudly for the small entryway. "Howya doin'?"

Oh my God. He's *loaded.* Can they tell? "We're just heading out the door, Dad. We'll see you later!"

He's ignoring me, looking at the boys now. "So, who are these strapping young lads?" He laughs like this is the funniest thing ever. I want to kill myself.

"This is Damian and Austin, Dad, but seriously, we've got to go. I'll see you later, okay?"

Dad's sizing up the boys. His eyes are unfocused and he leans a bit. Maybe the boys can't tell. Maybe it's only obvious to me.

"Well... hey, David. Justin. Nice to meet you. Erm... lemme shake your hand."

A little unbalanced, Dad starts across the entryway and puts out his right hand, but there's a glass of scotch in it, so he quickly tries to switch it over to his left hand, but he fumbles it somehow and then the glass is crashing to the floor, shattering, and scotch, ice cubes, and broken glass are spraying all over the place.

"Fuck!" my dad says. "Godammit!"

Everyone's standing there in shock, eyes wide, but Damian's the only one I care about. I can't believe he's seeing this. First time he's ever been to my house and he sees *this*.

Dad's down on one knee now, trying to fix things, but then he pulls up his hand and it's all bloody. "Jesus fucking Christ!"

If I were to fall over dead right now, that would be okay.

So Damian kneels down next to my dad, trying to

help, but I don't want him to. I *really* don't want him to. I just want him to leave. I want him to never have seen this.

"That's fine, Damian," I say, kneeling down next to him. "You don't have to do that."

"No, I can help," he says. "I don't mind."

"Oh, my fucking hand!" Dad says.

"No, no, no," I say. To nobody, to everybody. I feel like I'm about to burst into tears. "Just go, Damian. Please. I'm begging you."

Damian looks at me and seems to understand. Audrey's kneeling down, too, and she says, "You're sure? We can wait."

"No," I say to her. "Just go."

She stands and says, "Let's go, guys."

Damian stays down there with me for another second or two, not messing with the broken glass, but just looking at me. I'm too embarrassed to look back. I can only imagine what he's thinking. Finally, he stands up. "Okay," he says. "Um... It was nice to meet you, Mr. Blackman."

Dad's still on his knees, squeezing his bloody hand. When he looks up at Damian, it's like he's nine years old. "Um... yeah. Sorry. Shit. I'm so sorry, Maggie. Fuck."

I still can't look at Damian or the others. I just want them to leave so I can be alone in my nightmare. Eventually, they do. I think one of them says goodbye, but I honestly can't hear anything.

Once they're gone, I feel like putting my head in my hands and crying but I can't because I've got to clean up this mess. The entryway *reeks* of scotch, there's broken glass everywhere, and I've got this nine-year-old in front of me with a bloody hand.

Isn't this when a mom or a dad would swoop in and fix everything?

Not for me. I've got nobody. I'm completely on my own here.

Chapter 22

It turns out Dad needed stitches. I drove him to the hospital. He was super-apologetic and told me he was going to cut back on the drinking and I told him it was okay, but in truth, it's not okay at all, none of it's okay, and I think he knows that. It's been a week now and he hasn't gotten drunk again, so that's nice. It won't last much longer, but I guess I'll enjoy Sober Dad while I can. Not that I'm really enjoying him. I'm still pretty pissed at the guy. God, that was humiliating.

Thankfully, Audrey and Damian have been cool about it. Damian's been *more* than cool about it, actually. He called me later that night – first time he'd ever called me, by the way – and asked how I was doing and how Dad was doing and said all sorts of sweet and sympathetic things. Then he told me about how his mom gets drunk sometimes, too, which absolutely amazed me. It didn't amaze me that his mom gets drunk, just that he was willing to tell me about it. I swear, my crush on him is just through the roof now.

I wish he'd break up with Skyler already.

Of course, why would he do that? I don't actually know that he *likes* me. I sort of think he does – and Audrey's absolutely convinced – but that's not proof, is it? His being nice to me about Dad, that's not proof. Maybe he stays with Skyler because there's no one else he's interested in. Certainly not big, dopey, six-foot tall Maggie the Sasquatch.

Oh, well. Enough about that. The band is much less depressing and much more interesting. Today's the first practice with our brand-new guitarist, Emily Something-or-other. I can't remember her last name, but we're meeting at Aaron's. We're all going to squeeze into his bedroom and see what we can do.

I show up a little early and lug my stuff inside. With Aaron's drum kit and my big amp, there's not much room left, but Emily's small and so is her amp and when she gets there she just sets everything on Aaron's bed. We're chatting as we set up and I realize how little I know about her. I wouldn't say Aaron and I are best buds or anything, but we've sort of built a connection, all this time playing together. A musical connection, if nothing else. Now we've got to try and get that with Emily. It feels sort of like starting a new band.

"So I don't really know much about being in a rock band," she says as she's getting set up. "I was in the jazz band at my old school, but only for a few months."

Well, this gets Aaron all excited, of course, because he's in the jazz band, so they chat about that and I can see Emily relaxing a little.

"The only rock songs I know," she says to me, "are the songs you told me to learn. I hope that's okay."

"Totally okay. We'll go through them a bunch. It'll be plenty."

She looks relieved. "I was worried I'd be too Jazz Band Nerdy."

"Not with me here," Aaron says, raising a drumstick.

Emily has a small smile now. A nervous sort of smile. A nervous sort of I'm-just-happy-to-be-here-and-hope-I-don't-mess-this-up smile.

As I watch her, I can't help thinking about when I first pulled out my mom's bass and started trying to play. I showed up at David Nelson's barely knowing how to play a single song, and now look at me. Not only can I play, but I'm the leader of a band. A band this little sophomore girl is scared she's not good enough to be in. Amazing.

"Alright," I say. "Let's do this." And then the three of us start banging away at the few songs we know. We don't sound great, but we don't sound horrible, either. Emily's a little slow switching between chords, but otherwise, I like her. She's got a good attitude, she tries to keep her head up, her eyes on me and Aaron, and she doesn't mind playing the songs over and over, trying to get them down.

After an hour or so, we take a break and we're all standing around Aaron's kitchen, sharing this big jar of cashews his mom said we could finish. Emily's telling us about her old high school and the jazz band and how the teacher couldn't stand her because she barely knew how to play, and then she and Aaron start trading jazz band stories and it should be boring to me, but it's not because Emily turns out to be funny. I mean, the jokes she's cracking are stupid jazz band jokes, so I probably shouldn't be laughing, but still, I am. Here's one of her stupid jokes: how many trumpet players does it take to screw in a lightbulb? One, but he'll do it too loudly. See? Stupid. And here's another one: what did the drummer get on his IQ test? Drool. You see? There's no reason I should be laughing at these, but I am. It's nice to have a band practice with someone other than Josh. Instead of hateful comments, we get stupid jokes. Not a bad trade.

So we head back into Aaron's room – it's amazing his parents can put up with the noise we make – and go through the songs a few more times. We lost our microphone when we lost Josh, so I'm just singing as loud as I can. At a certain point, much to my surprise,

Emily starts singing along with me. With no microphone, it's a little hard to hear her, but I'm pretty sure she's in tune. And then, surprising me even more, *Aaron* starts singing, back there behind the drums, and that totally throws me, so I just stop playing and, after a second or two, they stop playing, too. It's quiet then and I ask Aaron why he hasn't sung before and he says he didn't think he was supposed to but then Emily did and it sounded good so he figured, why not? So we spend a few minutes just singing without music, trying to figure out how to do it properly, and Emily kind of knows a little about this, because she was in Chorus or something, and then, before you know it, we've sort of got this very rough three-part harmony thing going on. It's pretty cool, actually.

So we start playing again and this time we try to harmonize and it's fun and confusing and we keep messing up and have to start over but we're laughing the whole time and eventually we almost sort of get it right for a whole entire song and afterwards we're laughing and smiling and just having fun.

We keep at it another hour or so and by the time we finish I'm really quite happy with things. I mean, the music doesn't sound great – Emily's not nearly the guitar player Josh was – but I can tell she'll get better. And even more importantly, it feels like maybe we've got a better *band*, if that makes sense. Like this is the right group of people. Like we might actually enjoy each other, instead of just putting up with each other.

"Great first practice, Emily."

"Really?"

"Yeah," I say. "I think this is going to work out."

And that's pretty much our first practice with Emily. We make plans to meet again in a week, I give Emily a new song to learn, and then we're all smiles and optimism as we part ways.

The rest of the weekend is nothing special. I'm still angry at Dad, so we're not hanging out. If I were a better person, I'd probably sit down with him and tell him all the things I'm angry about and then make some sort of ultimatum or something. Stop drinking or else. That sort of thing. But of course, I don't do any of those things, because I'm a coward. And anyway, what ultimatum could I give him? Stop drinking or I'll move out? I'm not moving out. Where would I go?

I wish I were like the kids in the movies. The kids in books. They always know what to do. Me? I just stay in my room all weekend, moping around.

Monday at school is nothing special – just another Monday – but Audrey and I decide to go to Arleta's after school, so when the final bell rings, I go find her at her locker. As I'm standing there waiting for her, up walks Emily Stanwick. That's her last name, by the way. Stanwick.

"Hi, Maggie," she says, looking all nervous. "I just wanted to tell you that I've figured out that song, so I'm ready to go."

"Already?" I say. "It's only Monday."

"Yeah, well. I didn't have anything else to do yesterday. Oh, and I think maybe we can do the harmonies thing on it, too. I mean, if you want to, that is."

"Sure. Maybe. I'll have to listen to it, I guess, but maybe. I liked the harmony stuff we did."

"Me, too," Emily says. "I had so much fun on Saturday."

"Yeah?"

"Totally. It was the best time I've had in forever. Since I moved here, definitely."

Audrey finally has her stuff out of her locker, so she turns and introduces herself to Emily.

"Wow," Emily says. "Your hair's so cool." Audrey's hair is pink right now. A dark pink. Almost red. "I've thought about dying my hair, but I'm afraid to."

"Same for her," Audrey says, looking toward me. "Wants to dye it lilac, which I think would look pretty bad ass."

"That *would* look good," Emily says. "Are you

going to do it?"

"Maybe someday," I say.

"She's nervous," Audrey says.

"Maybe someday," I repeat.

Then, much to my surprise, Audrey says to Emily, "We're heading downtown to this vintage clothing shop. You want to come?"

Well, Emily says yes immediately, looking like she's going to explode with excitement. I'm kind of shocked Audrey asked her, since they just met 30 seconds earlier, but I can't say I mind. Actually, as the three of us walk out to the student parking lot and Audrey's beat-up old car, I become more and more glad that Emily's coming along. I mean, she's brand new in town and doesn't know anyone yet. Plus, she's my guitarist now. Maybe we could be friends, too.

In the parking lot, we see Aaron with some friends of his, all gathered around someone's car, messing around on their skateboards. He shouts over to us and waves and we all wave back and Emily says that he seems like a really nice guy.

"I'm so lucky," she says. "I get into my first rock band and everyone in it's just totally nice."

Well, that decides it. I'm going to make more of an effort to hang out with Aaron and Emily. To start thinking of them as friends, not just bandmates. It's not like I'm overflowing with friends, right? This will be good for me.

As we drive downtown, Audrey cranks up the stereo, playing this new band she's into. I'm not as sold on them, but they do have this one song I like and when it comes on, all three of us start singing along with it, loud as hell. Emily and I sort of try to harmonize a little, but it's hard doing it on the fly like that, with her in the back seat, me in the front, and Audrey just singing whatever, not trying to harmonize at all. Still, it's fun. I'm glad Emily came along.

Arleta's is fun. It's hard finding clothes that fit me, I'm so tall, but I find a nice belt and this cool red shirt. Emily's worried she's not cool enough to wear any of the stuff there, but we convince her to get one thing, a black skirt that would go with almost anything.

"You guys dress cool," she says.

"One word," Audrey says. "Vintage. And all your problems are solved."

"I'm actually not that cool," I tell Emily. "Audrey's been trying to cool me up a little."

Well, that starts us talking about me dying my hair and of course Audrey's totally ready and will do it for me that day, but I'm a coward and not ready and they tease me a little but not much.

Instead, we get coffee at the Bullfrog Cafe and talk

about boys and music and stuff, but mostly we just get to know Emily. And, yes, she's just a sophomore and I've only known her a week, but I'm feeling really good about her. She's nice. She's funny. She's smart. Plus, she's a good addition to the band. Sure, her guitar playing's only so-so, but with this harmonies thing she's got, well that really opens up some possibilities. To be honest, I'm feeling more optimistic about the band than I ever have before. We're really heading in the right direction.

But then Audrey drops me off at home and I'm walking up to the door when my phone rings.

It's David Nelson.

He wants me to join his band.

Chapter 23

The next day at school, I'm a wreck. I feel like a zombie, walking from class to class. My eyes are open and my feet shuffle along, but my mind isn't there at all. All I can think about is David Nelson and whether I should join his band.

His phone call could not have been a bigger surprise. Out of nowhere, really. I thought they'd broken up. Like, finished. Forever and ever. But no, it seems they managed to get their drummer back. Now they just needed a bass player.

But why would he ask me? I'm nothing. I can't play like Ty.

"Austin says you've gotten a lot better," he told me on the phone.

"Austin hasn't heard us."

"He hasn't?"

"No," I said. "Austin's full of crap. He's always full of crap. You don't know this?"

After a moment's pause, David said, "Well, it doesn't matter. I remember you from the auditions. You'll be fine."

So that's what I'm thinking about as I stumble blindly around school. David Nelson wants me. I have a chance to be in a great band. *The* great band. The best band at school. A band that actually plays for people. A band that's going to play the Follies in a couple months, in front of the whole school. I can be up there with them, sounding great, looking great, hearing that applause. The next day I'll be walking around school, people whispering about me, about how I'm going to be a star someday. I'll have people stopping me in the hallways to tell me how amazing I was. I'll have the cute guys after me. I'll have Damian after me.

So I have to do it, of course. I have to join David's band. There's no way I can do any of those things on my own. My stupid little band is never going to play parties. We're never going to play lunchtime concerts at school. We're never going to play for a packed auditorium at the Follies. The only way to do these things is with David.

In English class, Audrey can tell I'm not myself and she asks me what's up, but I just tell her I'm not feeling well. I don't think I can tell anybody about this. Not even Audrey.

And what should I do about Aaron and Emily? I'd just made the decision to become better friends with them. Now, a day later, I'm leaving them? Breaking up the band? Emily will be destroyed. She's brand new. My band is all she's got. Can I take that away from her? I'm not sure I can.

That night, I talk to my dad about it. It's early in the evening, so he hasn't had much to drink. Just the one scotch he always has when he gets home from work. There may be more later, I don't know, but for now, he's fine, we're making stir fry, and I'm asking him if Mom ever had to quit one band to join another.

"You're gonna quit your band?" he asks.

"No. Maybe. I don't know. Should I?"

I give him all the details and we finish cooking and sit down to eat and he makes himself another scotch, maybe because we're talking about Mom, maybe not. "She was in a few bands in high school," he says. "I'm not sure if she ever quit one of them. That was before I knew her. I don't know how those bands broke up."

"She was in a bunch of bands?" I ask, hoping he says yes, there were a million, they didn't mean anything to her.

"Well, not at the same time," he says. "But over the course of high school, yeah. Bands come and go, Maggie. Especially in high school. Nobody expects them to last forever."

We eat the stir fry and I think about this, wondering if Emily expects our band to last forever. Probably not. But I'll bet she expects it to last more than a week.

I wish I could think about all this for a few more days, but I can't, because David's band practices twice a week, once on Saturday and once on Wednesday night, which is tomorrow. So I've got to make a decision soon. Like, right now.

Dad and I clean up after dinner and he's getting a little drunk. Not a lot, but I can tell.

I screw up every bit of courage I have and say, "Um, Dad? Didn't you say you were going to drink less?"

Well, this does not go over well. Dad lets out a big sigh and says, "Jesus Fuckin' Christ, Maggie. I've had two drinks. Two. And with all the shit I put up with at work, excuse my language, I think I deserve a drink when I get home. I think I've earned it."

Well, that got me nowhere, so I just say, "Fine, fine, sorry I said anything," and head up to my room.

Lying on my bed, I pull out a notebook, open it to a clean sheet, and make a little chart. On the left side, I write: **David Nelson's Band**. On the right side: **My**

Band.

Over on David's side, I write: **Play parties. Play the Follies. Famous at school. Get Damian. Tons of cool friends.**

Over on my side, I write:

Well, actually, I don't write anything. Not at first. I can't think of anything.

Finally, I write: **Hang with Emily and Aaron**.

Then, after a second, I write: **No parties. No Follies. Nobody hears us. No Damian. No cool friends.**

I realize I sort of messed up that last part, so I scratch through ~~**No cool friends**~~ and write: **Only friends with Audrey**. Then, underneath it: **And maybe Emily and Aaron**.

I sit there on my bed for almost an hour, just imagining playing parties and being famous and having Damian as my boyfriend. Finally, I call David Nelson and tell him I'll do it.

“Cool,” he says. “Do you remember how to get to my house?”

I do remember, so David tells me to be there tomorrow at 7, then gives me a song to work on.

I know I should call Aaron and Emily, telling them the band's over, but I can't work up the courage, so I download the song David told me – it's a Ben Folds Five song, by the way – then head down into the basement and start trying to learn it.

It's an absolute bitch. Much harder than anything I've ever tried with my band. I've printed out a bass tab for the song, so that tells me the notes I'm supposed to play, but still, it's crazy-hard. As I sit there with my bass, trying to memorize this long, complicated bass line, rewinding the song over and over, I wonder if I've gotten myself in over my head. An hour passes, then two, and I'm still struggling. David's gonna want this song down perfect, but it's just crazy-complicated. The first part of the song is one thing, then it switches to something else, then back again, then something else entirely. And if that's not enough, it keeps changing speed! Slow, fast, slow, fast. God almighty! Who writes these things?

I eventually realize I need to write some of it down, so I go upstairs to get my notebook and when I look at the clock, it's way past time for bed. Still... fuck that. I need to to get this. I can't have David kicking me out of the band after one day. So I head back down to the basement and keep practicing and keep practicing and I never really get it down, but eventually I'm so tired I just can't do it anymore. I have to stop. When I finally collapse into bed, it's three in the morning. I forgot to call Aaron and Emily. Which may be a good thing. It's entirely possible David Nelson's going to hear me tomorrow and fire me on the spot.

Well, big surprise, I'm absolutely exhausted at school the next day. Even worse, I'm still all worked up over this band thing. The guilt, the uncertainty. I can't talk to anyone about it, not even Audrey. It's awful. I mean, I have a class with her in the morning and she's talking to me like everything's normal, and I'm just a big dumb idiot, hardly saying anything at all, because the only thing on my mind is this bitchin' hard song and David Nelson's band and I can't tell her anything about it.

Why can't I? Well, to be honest, I'm not sure. David didn't tell me it's a secret, so why am I treating it like one? I have no idea.

It isn't until lunchtime that I figure it out. Emily joins me and Audrey for lunch. It's a warm, sunny, perfectly gorgeous day, the kind of day that makes you think spring really has arrived, so half the school's out in the courtyard, including us. Everyone's laughing and soaking up the sun. Some guys near us are playing hackey sack. One of them has his shirt off.

Emily and Audrey are looking at the boys and deciding which ones are cute and which ones Emily should have a crush on and maybe go out with and I'm just sitting there all mopey, not saying anything. And then Aaron wanders up and he's with a couple friends and just wants to tell me he knows this dude who knows this other dude and that dude's got a couple mikes and mike stands and says we can use them on Saturday, and it would be awesome if we could get three mikes, so all of us could sing, but two's better than nothing, right? And Emily's agreeing and telling him how fun it's going to be and one of Aaron's friends starts flirting with her a little and Emily's blushing and Audrey's trying not to laugh and it's a gorgeous day and everyone's having fun and I can't enjoy a bit of it because I'm just wracked with guilt that I'm gonna be playing with David Nelson later that night.

And so *that's* why I'm keeping it all a secret. Because I'm ashamed. Ashamed that I'm doing this to Aaron and Emily. I can't tell them. I can't tell Audrey. Hell, I can barely tell myself.

Chapter 24

The last time I was at David Nelson's, it was dark and rainy and his house was surrounded by parked cars. Today, it's a whole different scene. No rain, no crowds, and it's still light when I get there, so I can actually see the place.

I lug my bass and amp out of the car and up to the door and Mrs. Nelson answers the bell and lets me in, still just as pretty as before.

Just like back in November, I head down into the basement, but this time there's no mobs of teenage girls, no cacophony of drums and guitar and talking and giggling. Actually, the place is pretty much empty except for two guys playing guitar. Austin and his dad.

"Maggie!" Austin says, turning to see me. "What

are you doing here?"

Standing there with my bass and my amp, I figure it's pretty obvious. "I'm here to play with David."

"You're kidding," Austin says, facing me now, an acoustic guitar hanging around his neck. "Audrey didn't tell me."

That's because she doesn't know, I think but don't say. *Because I'm a bad friend and ashamed of myself for coming here.*

David starts coming down the stairs then and he's got John Knowlson with him and they say hi and are pretty nice, I guess. John is, at least. David is a little standoffish. He shakes my hand, though, then sort of retreats over to his piano, where he sits and starts noodling around. His body's turned a little toward the room, and he's still watching me and the others, only playing with one hand, but he still sounds friggin' fabulous. It sounds like some sort of classical thing and he does it absently with his left hand, over and over, like he's not even thinking about it, like he's just exercising his fingers or something, but it's still more impressive than anything I can do on bass. The dude can really, really play.

"So," John says, standing there with me and Mr. Nelson and Austin. "You excited?"

No. I'm actually sort of terrified. "Sure. Can't wait."

"Awesome," John says. "Let's get started, then. Kieran should – Oh, here he is."

On the other side of the basement, coming in through a separate door, is Kieran, the drummer. I remember him and David arguing a little at the tryouts, but clearly they've worked it out. Enough that he's still in the band, at least.

The next few minutes are spent with all of us helping Kieran bring in his drum kit, then him setting it up, and then, before too long, we're ready to play.

David Nelson had been pretty quiet during most of that, but once we're ready to go, John shuts up and looks over to David, almost like he's handing over the role of leader. John was in charge before, but now that the music's starting, it's David.

Sitting at his piano, talking into the mike, David looks at me and says, "You've got that song down?"

I can't believe how nervous I am. I thought I was past all this. I'm the leader of a band, for crying out loud. I've fired guitarists! How can I come back to this basement and suddenly feel like it's Day One all over again and I'm a scared little girl, barely able to play her mom's bass?

Standing there, everyone looking at me, I manage to squeak out, "I think so," and then David nods at Kieran, who counts us off, and we start.

Well, first of all, I don't do too badly, so that's nice. This bass line is probably the hardest one I've ever tried – okay, *definitely* the hardest – but for the most part, I manage. I miss a few notes here and there – which David totally notices, I can see it on his face while he plays – but I never completely blow it and for that I'm grateful. First song with David Nelson and I don't make a complete fool of myself.

But more important than that, is this: the band sounds fabulous. Seriously. There is no comparison between this and what I've been doing with Aaron and Emily. We were just faking our way through some easy punk songs. These guys? These guys are *players*. Kieran's a hundred times better than Aaron, John's a thousand times better than Emily, and David? Oh, Lord. His playing. His voice. He's just... incredible. He doesn't even sound like a high school student. He sounds like he should be doing this professionally or something.

We get to the end and I'm thanking God I haven't messed up and my brain's swirling over how good that sounded and then it's quiet and everyone's just sort of waiting. John and Kieran are looking at David and he's looking at me and I'm starting to sweat, wondering what's getting ready to happen, and finally David leans forward and says into the mike, "Okay. Clearly that needs some work. But it could've been worse, I guess."

Well, I almost feel like I'm going to faint – I think I

was holding my breath or something, I'm so light-headed – but I'm smiling now, and I look over at John and he's smiling, too, and gives me a little wink, and so I'm feeling pretty good about things.

It doesn't last, though, because then David is talking again. He wants to go through the song again, but first he says to me, "You've got to get that bridge down. It's a pretty key moment in the song, so we can't have you missing it. Those are eighth notes, not quarter notes. Also, the chorus has a little drop step in it, and you're missing it every time. You need to stop there. Make sure you stop and muffle your strings, each and every time."

Well, I have no idea what half of that means, but I'm scared to say so, and every bit of good feeling I had just a second earlier is completely gone and I'm terrified again. Fortunately, John tells me I can watch him on the chorus, so I decide that's what I'm going to do, just watch John and try to ignore David, but when we go through the song again, David starts telling me to look at him. He does this as we're playing, which completely messes me up, but I look at him and almost get myself together, but then he's saying something else to me, something about the drop step, and I have no idea what's happening, I just feel like I'm getting yelled at, so I mess up really bad, and then David just stops playing and everyone else stops, too, and David curses into the mike and I'm afraid he's going to start screaming at me, but he doesn't, he takes a deep breath and waits a few seconds, then turns to me and starts lecturing me again, telling me in minute detail exactly what he wants.

Now, I'd love to tell you everything he says, but honestly, I don't understand half of it. It's all musician-talk and stuff I'd probably know if I'd ever taken a music lesson, but I haven't, have I? So I just sort of nod my head, glassy-eyed, and I'm not sure if David can tell, but John can, because he comes right up next to me and kind of shows me on his guitar what I should be doing on my bass and I nod and pretend I've got it, the whole time feeling completely out of my depth.

And that's pretty much how the rest of the evening goes. We practice for two hours and the whole time I'm just barely surviving, just barely keeping my head above water. The band sounds perfect to me, but clearly, to David's ears, we sound like a bunch of 4th-graders. By the time we finish, I'm sweaty, I'm exhausted, and I feel like someone's been sticking my finger in an electrical socket, over and over, all night. I want to crawl into a dark hole and never come out.

To make it worse, when I get home and turn my phone back on, there are three messages from Audrey, all of them basically the same. "What the hell are you doing, playing with David Nelson? How could you not tell me about this? Call me!"

I do call her, but it takes every bit of energy I have

and I feel like I want to cry, even before she picks up. I think she can tell, because she calms down pretty fast and stops yelling and agrees not to tell Aaron and Emily but I better tell her everything at school tomorrow, because that's what best friends do, dammit.

And then I shower and collapse into bed and I don't even eat or do my homework or download the songs David told me to learn. I just turn out the lights and bury myself in blankets and pretend I'm a hibernating bear, safe in my little burrow. Safe from music and basses and people giving me orders I can't understand, much less do.

Chapter 25

The next morning, I'm on the bus and John sits down with me and starts talking about the practice and how I did and I honestly don't want to hear a bit of it, I'm still a little frazzled, but I pretend I'm not and pretend I'm really excited about how things went and can't wait for Saturday when we can practice again.

Note to self, I think. *Cancel Saturday's practice with Aaron and Emily.* After a moment, I amend that mental note. *Move Saturday's practice to Sunday.*

"So, things are looking good," John says as we bounce along, heading to school. "Robbie McMorrison wants us to play his graduation party. Add that on to Marjorie Cooper's party the week before, plus the Follies the week before *that*, and we're gonna be pretty busy."

"We're playing at Robbie McMorrison's?" I say in disbelief.

Robbie McMorrison's, like, the most popular guy at our school. He's a senior, obviously, and if he's throwing a graduation party, it's gonna be huge. People like me don't go to his parties. We don't even *hear* about his parties.

"Yeah," John says. "That's new. We already knew about Marjorie's party. And the Follies, of course, but that's just three songs."

Just three songs. *Just* three songs. Last night, *one* song practically put me into a coma. Three songs might kill me. And God know how many songs I'll have to learn if we play Robbie McMorrison's party.

I'm pretty quiet the rest of the way to school.

Once we're there, I don't even make it to my locker before Audrey pulls up alongside me. I'm worried she's going to start demanding information, but she doesn't, probably because I look so close to breaking. Instead, she just walks with me, no questions, no demands. It's so sweet, I almost want to burst into tears. God, I'm a wreck, aren't I?

"So, don't worry," she finally says quietly as we walk down the noisy hallway. "I told Austin not to tell anyone."

"Thanks."

"And you don't have to tell me until you're ready."

"Thanks."

"But I really do want to know."

"Okay."

"When you're ready."

"Thanks."

"Maybe during English."

"Mmh."

"Or lunch."

"Mmh."

"Whenever."

And then she's off, heading to her first-period class, waving over her shoulder. I feel so lucky to have her as a friend. I guess I'll tell her at lunch.

Except when lunch finally comes, Emily's there, so I can't say anything, but honestly, I sort of forget about it because Emily's just out of her mind excited, telling us about this boy who called her last night. He didn't ask her out, but she thinks he wants to and she hopes he does. So then Audrey and I are all, like, you should ask *him* out, and that gets us talking about when I asked Diego out, though maybe that's not the best example, since we all know how that turned out, but it doesn't really matter, because the point is, Emily's being so cute and funny that I'm in a much better mood now and can almost forget about the whole band mess for awhile. And then, best of all, we're out there in the courtyard eating – it's not as warm as the other day, but it's still pretty nice – and who races up but Austin and Damian and DeAndre. They're in class, but the teacher is walking the whole class to the library or something, and they see us and race over, I mean literally *run*, and it actually surprises us, them coming out of nowhere like that, and Austin plants a big kiss on Audrey's cheek and she shrieks a little, she's so surprised, and then Damian – I swear to God this is true, I'm not making this up – he gives *me* a big smooch on *my* cheek, and I know he was just being funny, but who cares, right? He still kissed me! And then DeAndre keeps it going and kisses Emily on *her* cheek, and I don't think he's even *met* Emily, so she shrieks and laughs, her face bright red, and then the three boys are racing away to catch up with their class and we're sitting there laughing and blushing and I'm just about beside myself because Damian kissed me, even if it was just for a laugh, so then Emily gets to hear all about me and Damian and the whole pathetic story and it's fun to just be gossiping like a normal girl, not a girl who's got a dead mom and a drunk dad and is getting ulcers from trying to hide the fact that she's in two bands. And when lunch is over and we're saying goodbyes, Emily gives both me and Audrey hugs, like we're old friends, and she's like 5'4", tops, so it's probably a little ridiculous-looking, her hugging big old six-foot me, but it's still really nice. It makes me feel like I actually have *friends*, plural, and I'm just really glad she moved to town and we met.

Well, that afternoon, when school lets out, instead of taking the bus home, I ride with Audrey to her house and tell her the whole David Nelson story. I don't enjoy it. We're walking around Audrey's neighborhood with her dog Blackie, soaking up the weak springtime sun, and just the process of telling Audrey the story makes my body tighten up, my face turn gloomy.

"Are you sure you want to be in his band?" Audrey says. "You don't act like it."

I'm a little surprised by her question. "Well, I mean, of *course* I want to. They're fantastic. You should hear them."

"I have heard them," Audrey says. "They're great. But is that what you want?"

"Well, yeah. I mean... there's the parties and the... I don't know, the *boys*. Don't you think Damian would want to go out with me if I was in David Nelson's band?"

"I think Damian already wants to go out with you."

"Well, enough to dump Skyler, then. I mean, it's *the* band. Don't you think?"

"I don't know, sweetie. I don't think Damian really

cares about all that. Maybe. I just know you seem miserable. That's all."

I don't really have anything to say to that because I'm pretty sure she's right. I do wonder, though, exactly *why* I'm miserable. Is it because David's band is so much harder? Or is it the guilt that's killing me? The guilt of keeping it a secret from Emily and Aaron. Maybe if I told them, I'd instantly feel better. Maybe if I told them, broke up our band, and dedicated myself to David's, I'd feel good again.

I could do that. I could call them right now. My phone's in my pocket. Maybe all this tension and misery would just disappear.

Audrey and Blackie and I walk around her neighborhood in silence. It's a big circle, her neighborhood, and in the middle is a swimming pool and community clubhouse. "When do they open the pool?" I ask.

"Oh, I'm not sure," she says. "A month, maybe? I wish they opened it earlier. I wish it were open now. We could be swimming right now."

"A little cold, don't you think?"

"Nah. I love swimming. I'd do it all winter, if it was an indoor pool."

"What about the clubhouse?" I ask her.

"Oh, that's open. That's always open."

"What do they use it for?"

"Different stuff. Meetings. Parties. I went to a birthday party there once. I think I was eight. There was a magician and everything. I can't remember whose party it was. Barbara Felton, maybe. She used to live here."

I end up having dinner with Audrey and her moms. We don't talk about my band problems, but it's on my mind. My phone's still in my pocket. I could call Emily and Aaron, break up the band, and put this whole thing behind me. All of this guilt would just be over. I'd be happy again.

Or would I? I have no idea.

So I don't call. I just go home and practice the new songs David told me to learn. No surprise, they're brutally hard and I go to sleep exhausted and stressed and sick of music.

Chapter 26

I don't call Emily and Aaron. I don't tell them at school the next day. I see plenty of them, of course. We hang out a little at school. I change Saturday's practice to Sunday. Talk with them about the band. Talk about stuff that's not the band. But during none of that am I able to tell them it's over. Tell them I'm leaving them. Moving on.

So now it's Saturday and I'm at David Nelson's and he's all pissed off about something else I've done wrong and I don't even understand half of what he's saying. Something about "eighth-notes" and how I'm hitting it on the "and-three," when I'm *supposed* to be hitting it on the "three-and."

You see what I'm dealing with here? He might as

well be speaking Japanese.

Audrey's here. Officially, she's here for Austin, but she's been watching our practice, too. Right now, she's sitting on that awesome leather sofa, leafing through a magazine. She taps her foot along with the music, stops tapping while David tells me everything I'm doing wrong.

"Okay, we've run that one into the ground," David says into his microphone. "It's close, though. Let's do 'Let It Be.' Maggie, you figured out your vocal part, right?"

"Erm... I think so?"

That's about as certain as I can get here. Yes, I figured out my vocal part. But, no, it won't be the way David wants it. Nothing I do is the way David wants it.

So we roll into the song. It sounds good. These guys are so solid, they make even me sound better.

David stops us halfway through so he can tell me what I'm doing wrong.

We start the song again. Again, we sound good. We're singing some nice harmonies, similar to what we've started doing in my band.

Wait. My band? Isn't *this* my band now? It's confusing to think about, so I focus back on the song.

David stops us again so he can tell me again what

I'm doing wrong.

And so on and so on. It's demoralizing.

Making it even worse? I don't even like the songs that much. I feel kind of bad saying that, since I mean, who doesn't like the Beatles? And Ben Folds? He's great. Clearly, we're playing "good songs."

Okay, I'm gonna back up. It's not that I don't *like* the songs. I do. It's that it's no fun playing them. They're slower, mellower. I sort of miss the punk songs I play with Aaron and Emily. They're upbeat, they're high energy, they're fun. Playing music should be fun, right?

We're going through the song yet again when Austin comes waltzing in. He's shirtless and sweaty from playing basketball out in the driveway. He's got Damian and DeAndre with him. They're shirtless and sweaty, too.

Repeat: I'm in the same room with a shirtless and sweaty Damian Shaw. And, yes, he looks good. You bet your ass he looks good. A little meat on his bones, but not too much. Decent muscles, but not too much. He's even got a little six-pack going. Not all rock-hard chiseled stone, but still, just a little. Enough so you can see it's there.

Well, whatever chance I had of making it through this song is completely gone now. They're over by the bar, getting water, and I'm looking at Damian, totally messing up my bass line.

David stops us and I jump in before he can say anything. "Um, David? Could we take a break, maybe? Just a few minutes?"

From behind the drums, Kieran says, "Yeah, I gotta take a leak." He doesn't wait for David, just gets up and walks off. David looks annoyed, but there's not much he can do.

"Okay," he says, rising from his piano. "Ten minutes. Then we get back on this."

I put down my bass and collapse next to Audrey on the couch.

"Poor baby," she says, patting my head. "Beatles songs make baby grumpy."

"Don't taunt the baby," I say, lying there, eyes closed. "The baby is friggin' exhausted."

I hear John putting up his guitar, chatting with David as they go upstairs. Finally, it's quiet, but I stay there on the couch, eyes closed. I need a short break. A few minutes of peace, with no one telling me what I'm doing wrong. I can tell Audrey's still sitting next to me, but she's silent, for which I'm thankful. I've sort of forgotten about the boys, so I'm a little startled when I hear Damian speak from just a few feet away.

"You need to get out of this band, Maggie."

My eyes open wide and there he is in front of me, shirtless, leaning against an amplifier.

"What?"

"You need to get out of this band."

Looking around the basement, I see it's just the three of us. Don't know where Austin and DeAndre went.

Up by my head, Audrey says, "Cut her some slack, Damian. She's just had David all over her ass. You think she needs you, too?"

"Well, that's the problem, isn't it?" Damian says. "David all over her ass." To me, he says, "You don't need this. You've got a band of your own. A good band."

"Not this good," I say.

"Who cares?" he says. "You're clearly not having fun. What do you need this crap for?"

Again, Audrey steps in. "Shut up, Damian. Don't listen to him, Maggie. Let's go get you some food or something. He's an idiot."

We stand and head up the stairs. Damian follows behind. Putting his shirt back on, unfortunately.

"I'm not an idiot," he says. "I just think you're happier in your own band. And I don't like David yelling at you."

"He doesn't yell," I say.

"You know what I mean," he says from behind me. "I don't like it."

But then we go through the door at the top of the stairs and everyone's right there in the kitchen, so we shut up. I get a glass of water and everyone's sharing a big bowl of grapes so I have some of those. The kitchen and the living room are all sort of one big room, but it still feels busy, what with the four musicians, plus the three basketball players, plus Audrey. Damian's right there next to me, both of us leaning against the kitchen counter. I'm painfully aware of how our shoulders press together. I lower my arm to my side and our hands touch, which is both wonderful and terrifying. I wish I could hold his hand. It would be so easy. I could just slip my hand into his, like it's the most normal thing in the world. I'm not even sure people would notice. Damian would notice, though, so I can't do it.

On the other side of the room, Austin and DeAndre stand up from the kitchen table and start toward the front door. Heading back to their basketball hoop, I assume. “Let's do it,” DeAndre calls out to Damian.

“I'll be there in a second,” Damian says and takes a sip from his water glass, then leans down a little and says quietly, so only I can hear, “I'm gonna call you later. I don't think you should be in this band.” And then he heads across the room and out the door.

Once he's gone, Audrey comes over and she and I start whispering about Damian and what he said and I'm all excited about his calling later, even though it's only so he can yell at me about the band. "Do you agree with him?" I whisper to Audrey. "About the band?"

She sighs and doesn't answer right away, looking uncomfortable. Finally, she says, "I want you to be happy."

This isn't an answer, of course, which is annoying. Especially since I think it means she wants me in my old band, which means everybody's against me now.

We're silent for another few minutes, then David says, "Okay, break's over," and we all head back downstairs. Everyone but Audrey, who says she's going to go watch the boys play ball. I give her a dirty look. I feel like she's abandoning me. Damian, too.

The last half of practice is pretty much the same as the first half. We work through these really difficult, not terribly fun songs. Everything sounds great to my ears, but David keeps stopping us and telling us what we're doing wrong. And when I say "us," what I really mean is "me."

When we get to the end of the practice, I'm packing up my stuff and David comes up to me and tells me I'm doing a good job.

"You've got a lot of potential," he says. "You could be great. But you're only going to get there if you really dedicate yourself. You need to practice more, you need to commit to becoming great. And, also... you're going to have to choose a band. You can't do this two-band thing anymore. You need to make a choice."

Yeah. So that's what I get to think about as I'm heading home. Big Decision Time. It's just fun, fun, fun in the life of Maggie Blackman, isn't it?

When I get home, I'm exhausted and demoralized and want nothing more than a shower and a nap, but Dad meets me at the door, eager to have the car back so he can go to the store. "And you're coming with me, sweetie. I need help with the bags."

This is the absolute last thing I want to do right now. I tell Dad how exhausted I am, but he's unimpressed. "It'll just be a few minutes," he says. "Especially if there's two of us."

Well, big surprise, it's more than a few minutes – much more – because once we're on the road, Dad remembers a few other things he wants to do, so after the grocery store, he's running into the hardware store for God knows what, plus there's the post office, and then we're stopping at the bank so he can run in for just a second.

I'm completely annoyed by all this, of course, but it's a pretty day, and after the long winter, any bit of sunshine seems like a gift, so I wait for him on this little bench in front of the bank, my eyes closed and my face up to the sun.

"Hey, good lookin'."

I open my eyes and who's standing there but Damian Shaw. "Are you following me?" I ask him.

"Yeah. And you're making it pretty easy, too. You should wear camouflage or something. Hide in the bushes."

"What are you doing here?"

"The bank. Need some cash. What about you?"

"My dad's inside. He roped me into coming along. I just wanted to take a nap."

Just then, Dad comes walking out. "Hey, who's this?" he says.

Before I can say anything, Damian puts out his hand and says, "Hi, Mr. Blackman."

"Nice to meet you," he says, shaking Damian's hand. "What's your name?"

Damian gives me a very quick look, a look that says, *He doesn't remember meeting me that day, does he?* "It's Damian. Damian Shaw."

"You friends with Maggie?"

"Yes, sir. Best friends. She doesn't talk about me all the time?" Damian shakes his head at me. "That hurts, Maggie. It really does."

Dad has a good laugh, then asks Damian if he's heading into the bank and then – I'm not quite sure how – they're somehow talking about basketball. Dad used to play, of course, so they're comparing teams and positions and coaches and I don't know what all, but I'm just sitting there watching it all and it's sort of amazing, actually. They're talking and laughing and... I don't know. I guess I'd just forgotten my dad could be so *normal*. It's really nice. He's just being a *dad*, you know? Not a drunk dad. Not a sad dad. Just a dad. Talking with one of my friends. The boy I have a crush on.

So I'm really enjoying all this normalcy, but then Dad has to ruin it by saying, "Well, Damian, we've got to get going, but you feel free to come by the house anytime, okay? Actually, that would be perfect. Are you watching the playoffs? Maggie won't watch with me."

"Dad!"

"What?"

"Damian's not going to come to the house so you two can sit around watching basketball!"

"What? Why not? I was just..."

"Dad, stop it! You're embarrassing me!"

Well, this just makes Dad laugh and then Damian's laughing, too, so of course, I'm absolutely mortified and want to kill them both, but then Dad finally shuts up and shakes Damian's hand and tells me it's time to go and we start for the car, but Damian says, "Actually, could I talk to Maggie for just a second? It'll just be a second, I swear."

So Dad heads to the car and Damian says, "Listen, about earlier."

"The band," I say, rolling my eyes.

"Yes, the band. You're miserable in there, Maggie. And you know it."

Standing there, I suddenly feel beyond tired. I shut my eyes and take a deep breath. I'm trying to think what I should say to him, but there really isn't much to say, is there? Because he's right.

This is all so exhausting. I wish I could just put my head on his chest and let him hug me. Would he do that? Wrap his long arms around me and just hold me?

I still haven't said anything, just standing there with my eyes closed, so Damian says, "And anyway, you shouldn't be taking orders from David. You should be the one giving the orders. Like you do in your band. You're so much cooler in there."

"My band's not cool," I say, finally opening my eyes. "David's band is cool."

"David's band is *better*, but they're not cooler."

"You think I'm cool?"

"Well, not when you're in there with David. Then, you're just another musician, taking orders. But in your own band, yeah. You're cool when you're doing *your* thing. Not David's thing. That's what makes you cool."

We stand there in front of the bank for a little bit, not really saying anything. There's nothing else to say. Eventually, he heads into the bank and I head back to the car. When we pull out of the parking lot and head towards home, Dad says, "Damian seems like a hell of a guy. Why aren't you two dating?"

I can only shake my head and give a sad chuckle. *If you only knew, Dad. If you only knew.*

Chapter 27

So the next day is Sunday and I sleep late as hell. By the time I get up and get dressed and get fed, it's pretty much time for practice. That's my life these days. If I'm not practicing with one band, I'm practicing with the other.

Will I be able to tell them today? Tell Aaron and Emily I'm leaving them for another band? It's time to make the decision. David Nelson's orders.

Should I wait for the end of practice? I shouldn't, should I? That would just be cruel. Have an entire practice for no reason? I should do it at the beginning. Maybe I should just call. Not even go. No, I should go. I should do it face-to-face. That's the right way to break up a band, I guess. Not that I've ever done this before. With Josh, I just kind of yelled a lot, then stormed out. This isn't the same thing at all. I like Aaron and Emily. I just need to break up with them.

Sigh.

Deep, heavy sigh.

This sucks.

I don't know why I even bother taking my bass and my amp, but I do. And then I haul them out of the car and up to Emily's front door, which seems stupid if I'm just going to kill the band, but whatever, I do it anyway.

I don't really get a chance to kill the band, though, because as soon as Emily opens her front door, she's howling with laughter and pulling me inside and freaking out about something, I'm not even sure what, but she's practically falling down, she's laughing so hard. And Emily's laughter is always so contagious, so pretty soon I'm laughing along with her, trying to figure out what the hell she's on about and I've forgotten all about the band stuff.

So, anyway, what's got Emily going is definitely worth laughing about. It's almost hard to believe, actually. It turns out that right before I rang the doorbell, she got a call from this boy named Richie and he asked her out on a date. Which is cool, I guess, but that was only *after* this boy named Travis also called her this morning and also asked her out on a date, and I'm like, you're kidding me, and she's like, no I'm serious, I swear to God. So I'm like, who has two separate boys call her on the same day and ask her out on dates and she's like, I know, right? This has never happened to her before, that's why she's laughing so hard, because she's not used to one boy asking her out, much less two, but then she *really* starts laughing and tells me that, she swears to God this is true, but last night, Saturday night, a *third* boy called her, a boy named Simon, and I'm like, okay, this isn't real, this is like something from TV or something, and she is literally on the floor laughing, holding herself, trying not to pee her pants. Well, that's when the doorbell rings and it's Aaron, so that *really* gets us laughing and he's like, what, what, but there's no way we're telling him, which pisses him off, but whatever, he's a boy, so Emily and I are giggling and whispering as we haul all my stuff and all Aaron's stuff into her garage. I'm asking her if this is normal life for her and she says no, she's never even had a boyfriend, much less *three* of them, so she doesn't know what to do and I certainly don't know what to tell her, I've only had Diego.

Well, we finally cave and tell Aaron about it, so then he's laughing and amazed and says he knows Simon and Travis, but not Richie, and he can't believe she had three people ask her out, he'd settle for just one. Emily completely agrees and says it must be because she's new or something, because she's never even been on a date, much less had a boyfriend, so she doesn't know what to do, does he have any advice? Well, I guess we're all in a confessional mood because Aaron tell us he's only gone out with one girl and that was only for a month, so he's not sure it counts, but if he had to pick one of those guys for Emily he'd pick Simon, because Travis is kind of a dick sometimes and he doesn't even know Richie, not really.

So by this point we're all set up in Emily's garage and start to play.

And it's great.

Seriously. It's so great.

I mean, it doesn't *sound* as good as it did at David Nelson's. Our playing isn't as good, my voice isn't as good as David's, and the songs aren't as complex or impressive, but none of that matters. This just *feels* right. We're playing this Green Day song and it's fast and loud and fun. We're doing the whole harmonizing thing, but we've only got two mikes, so we've given one of them to Aaron, while Emily and I share the other one, and I know it doesn't sound as good as the sound system at David's, and I'm sure our harmonies aren't as good, but who cares? We're having fun! We're singing and smiling and enjoying ourselves. And even though there are a few problems along the way, when we get to the end of the song, I don't even make us go back and play it again. I'm in too good a mood and want to immediately play another one. So we roll into this New Found Glory song we learned last week and it's just the same as with the last one. Not perfect, but...

somehow... perfect.

Practices with David felt like something to survive. Playing with Aaron and Emily feels like coming home.

We roll straight through our entire repertoire – which isn't a lot, really. Just seven songs – and it's totally fun. We talk a little about some harmony stuff we could do on one of the songs, then Aaron shows us this new thing his drum teacher showed him. It's this cool kick drum thing, and so he's playing it and then Emily starts strumming her guitar along with it and so I figure, why not, and start playing along with it, too. We just keep rolling and we're cooking along pretty good, just doing stuff on the fly and, when we finish, Emily's like, "Wait... did we just write our first song?"

"I guess we did," I say, smiling.

"Awesome!" Aaron says, all sweaty behind his drum kit. "Let's cut an album!"

"When do we go on tour, boss?" Emily says to me.

"We'll need a bus," I say.

"Two buses," Aaron says. "Boys and girls."

"Fine," Emily says. "All my boyfriends can ride on your bus."

So there we are, all sunshine and optimism, and then I get an idea and say to them, "But, seriously, guys. We should play a party."

"Play music?" Aaron says. "At a party?"

"That's the idea."

"People do that?" he says.

"Could *we* do that?" Emily says.

"Sure we could," I say. "We've got seven songs. Eight, if you count our original."

"You need more than that to play a party," Emily says. "Don't you?"

I have no idea. None of us do. We've never been to a party with a band. That's what cool people do. We're not cool.

We talk for awhile, wondering if anyone we know is having a party. Do we know people who have parties? My only friends are Audrey and the two people in this room. Damian, I guess. Austin and DeAndre maybe a little.

Wait. Audrey! She's got that clubhouse! With the pool!

I immediately call her up and tell her my plan.

"You're gonna quit David's band? Oh, I'm so glad!"

"Yeah, me, too. So, can we have a party at your clubhouse?"

"I don't really know," she says. "I've never rented it out. I'm not even sure kids are allowed to. I'll talk to my mom.”

So we hang up without really deciding anything, but whatever, it's still fun thinking about it. Thinking we might actually play a party.

But best of all, it's good to be decided. To know that I'm in this band. My band, not David's. With people I like. With Aaron and Emily. My friends.

Chapter 28

The next few weeks are excellent. I can't quite believe it, but my life actually seems good again. Spring is here, it's warm and sunny, and everything seems to be falling into place for one Maggie Blackman.

Oh, sure, David was a little annoyed when I told him I was staying with my old band, but he got over it. I don't think losing me is what upset him, to be honest. He just didn't want to go searching for another bassist. But whatever. I'm not letting it worry me. I've had all the David Nelson-related stress I need, thank you.

Things are good on the Dad front, too. He got offered a new position at work, which he was super-excited about. Plus, he's hardly drinking at all these days. It's so great. Maybe it was dropping that glass and cutting his hand that helped him turn the corner. Maybe it was me giving him the cold shoulder for weeks afterward. Or maybe he's just getting over Mom dying. I know the pain's faded for me. I still miss her and I still get sad, but it's not like before. I'm not bursting into tears all the time. Maybe it's the same for Dad. Whatever the reason, it's nice to have him back. Nice to spend evenings with him, just a father and a daughter. I'm even willing to watch some of his stupid sports games.

Damian? Well, hmm... no changes there, I'm sad to report. I mean, he's still awesome, and we still hang out, and I still think maybe he likes me, but a lot of good all that does me. He still has a stupid little blond girlfriend who goes to South Sycamore. I'll admit, he doesn't seem all that happy with her, but whatever. I should probably start looking for another guy. Diego Alva, part two.

The band is kicking ass. We're practicing twice a week now and trying to add a bunch of new songs. Aaron even went out and got another mike. It's the idea of playing a party that's really lit a fire under us.

Not that we've actually got a party yet. It's still just an idea. And that's why we're sitting at the Bullfrog Cafe, drinking iced lattes and making plans. It's the whole band, plus Audrey.

"So we got it for Saturday?" Aaron says.

"Yes," Audrey says.

"Do we get the clubhouse *and* the pool?" Emily asks. "Or just the clubhouse?"

"Both," Audrey says. "Though we don't really *get* the pool. It's open to everybody, just like always. But the clubhouse is ours."

We talk for awhile about whether we should do it during the day or during the night – we can sunbathe during the day, but swimming at night is also kind of cool. Plus, Aaron says at night we can go skinny dipping, which I can assure you is definitely *not* happening – and then we start talking about swimsuits and where we can get cute bikinis, at which point Aaron completely checks out.

The party's two weeks away, on the first weekend the pool's open and two weeks before school lets out. It's also the night after the North Sycamore Follies. We're not playing that show, of course, but David's band is, so it seems noteworthy. We're all going, of course. Everybody goes. It's a huge thing, completely filling the school auditorium. All sorts of kids get up on stage, doing all sorts of stuff. Comedy stuff, dancing stuff, music stuff. Last year, this boy did this whole acrobatics thing. Flips and handstands. It was actually pretty cool. Or maybe it just seemed cool because he was our age and he had a bunch of friends in the audience cheering him on. Anyway, David's band will be playing.

They did find a bass player, by the way, but he's not from our school. He's a college kid, I think. I don't know how David found him, but I assume he's good, since he's so much older. I'm really looking forward to seeing them. I wonder if it'll be hard to watch, since I'll know it could've been me up there.

Well, I'm not going to sweat that. I'm happy with my decision. And we've got a gig that weekend, too. If we can get it organized.

“Okay, listen now,” Audrey says. “No more joking. We've got to get as many people there as we can. Now, Emily, you don't really know a lot of people. Are you sure there's no one you can invite?”

“My little sister?”

“God, no,” Audrey says.

“Yes!” Aaron says. We give him quizzical looks, so he adds sheepishly, “She's kind of hot.”

“Jesus Christ, Aaron!”

“What? She is!”

“She's a freshman!”

“Fine. She'll be a sophomore next year. Tell her to bring her friends. We need people.”

“I don't want my little sister there.”

“Do you want this party to be empty?” Aaron says. “Beggars can't be choosers. We need people.”

"What about Simon?" I ask Emily. "He can probably bring a bunch of people."

Emily's dating Simon now. She's happy to have a boyfriend, but I don't think they're in love or anything. Still, he's got friends, they've got friends. If we're going to have a good party, we need to work our connections, which is sort of a problem, since none of us run with the cool crowd.

I remember when Audrey and I first became friends. I thought she was so cool back then. I thought she had tons and tons of friends and they were always doing cool stuff together, stuff I couldn't even imagine. But in truth, she's just like me. Just a girl trying to figure things out. Trying to get through each day. Only with cooler clothes. And green hair.

The four of us keep at it until we've got a pretty good plan for who to invite. I think our best chance for filling the party is getting the basketball team to bring friends.

And right then, as if on cue, Audrey's phone rings and it's Austin. Audrey's side of the conversation goes something like this:

"Hey, sweetie! At the Bullfrog, where are you? Yes, I'm sitting down, why? Okay. Just tell me already. No! You lie! When? Ohmigod. So it's official? It's done? Ohmigod. He's with you? No! When? Okay, I'll tell her. Bye."

When she hangs up, her eyes are wide and she says, "Damian broke up with Skyler!"

All around me, hell breaks loose. Audrey and Emily are freaking out, shrieking and giggling and clutching each other. Aaron's trying to quiet them down so we don't get kicked out, but even he's smiling at the news, looking at me with wide eyes.

What am I doing? Nothing, really. I'm paralyzed.

"They're coming here!" Audrey says. "Austin said they're, like, two minutes away. Maybe less."

Oh my God, oh my God, oh my God.

"I can't be here," I say, standing up from the table. "I've got to go."

"The hell you do!" Audrey says, grabbing my arm and pulling me back into my seat. "You're not going anywhere!"

"I have to. I can't stay here. Please let me go. Please. I can't be here. I can't."

"Tough," Audrey says. She won't let go of my arm. "You're going to be here and you're going to ask him out on a date."

Oh, dear Jesus, I have such a panic attack then, I'm surprised I don't turn into the Hulk or something. I'm ready to dive through the cafe's plate glass window. "Let me go, let me go. I can't do this."

"You're doing this!"

Well, that's when I hear the little bell tinkle because the front door's opened and Audrey's letting go of my arm and saying, "Well, hey guys! Come on in! Good to see you! Hi, *Damian*!"

I'm a stone statue, sitting there, eyes wide, staring at my iced latte. No part of me can move. I sort of hear people talking and I'm vaguely aware that people are sitting down at our table, but mostly I'm just locked in on my drink, brain completely shut down. My face is on *fire*.

When everyone has sat down and settled in, there's quiet. But not a good quiet. An uncomfortable quiet.

Audrey sips her drink and says, "So, guys, what's shakin'?"

There's a pregnant pause, then Austin says, "Not much. Just bummin' around." Another pause, then he adds, "Might go to the park."

I'm looking down at my glass, but I'm sure everyone's staring at me. I feel like I'm going to burst into flames.

Audrey says, "What about you, Damian? Anything new?"

I could kill Audrey right now. I sneak a peek at Damian. He's looking down at his lap, his face red. We're like two peas in a pod. I wish everyone would just leave us alone. Wait, check that. I don't mean people should actually *leave.* God, can you imagine? Just me and Damian? I think I'd die.

"Erm... not much," Damian says. The poor guy looks as bad as me. "Just... you know, hanging out. Like Austin said." He sneaks a quick glace at me, catches me looking at him. I immediately look at my drink again, mortified.

There's more horrible silence, then Emily says, "Nice day, isn't it?"

People nod their heads. I stare at my latte. This is so awful. Can I run from the room right now? Is that allowed? What about setting myself on fire? Can I do that, too?

Well, this goes on for another... I don't know... five hours. Finally, Austin says, "Well, I guess we'll get out of here, then."

Audrey's like, "Oh. You're sure? You can stay. Damian, don't you want to stay?"

I sneak a peek at Damian and he's sneaking a peek at me and we catch each other doing it and it's awful and I look back at my drink and he says, "Um, well, no, I guess we should probably go."

Yes! Go! Leave before I sweat through my shirt.

So they say their goodbyes and I'm silent. As soon as they're out the door, Audrey's all over me, giving me crap about not talking to Damian and I'm giving her crap right back about embarrassing me and Emily's like, why can't you talk to him, you guys are friends, and Aaron's mostly just making fun of us.

"You need to call him right now!" Audrey says, pointing her stupid finger at me. "You need to ask him out!"

"I'm not asking him out!" I say, glaring at her. We're not exactly screaming at each other, since we're at the Bullfrog and other people are here, but you know how it is. We're whisper-shouting. "He doesn't want to go out with me! You saw him!"

Well, dear God, this just sends everyone into a fit and they're all blah blah blah-ing and whatever.

In the end, I tell them all to shut up and leave me alone about it and Audrey's all mad at me, but we finally force ourselves to get back to organizing the party. Or at least they do. My mind's not in it. I'm thinking about Damian and how awful this whole thing is.

Why did he have to break up with Skyler? Everything was so easy when he had a girlfriend. I was crazy for him, he was taken, end of story. See? Easy.

But now what do I do? He's single, so... so *what*, exactly? What do I do?

I feel like I'm going to throw up.

Chapter 29

Monday.

Science to English.

I'm at my locker, freaking out. Actually, let's be honest, I started freaking out halfway through Science class. Now, here I am, getting my books, absolutely paralyzed with fear because Damian's getting ready to come down that hall and walk my stupid ass to English.

And he's *single*.

There's no way we can avoid this. We didn't talk at the Bullfrog, but we'll have to talk now. We'll *have* to.

Oh, God, this is going to be horrible. I can't even look. I face my locker, trembling. Behind me, the normal hallway chaos goes on, oblivious.

Finally, I hear someone clear his throat. "Um... Maggie?" It's Damian. His voice is almost a squeak.

I turn and face him. I can barely look up. "Hi."

We stand there for a couple seconds, neither of us quite able to make eye contact. Finally, I turn and start down the hall toward English. He pulls up alongside me.

I have never felt so awkward in my life. I'm walking like a robot, stiff and clumsy. Next to me, Damian is silent. I can't look at him.

When we get to my classroom, I say goodbye and rush inside. I don't look back.

I collapse into my seat and exhale. Dear God, I am the most pathetic person in the world. The whole entire world.

Tuesday.

I'm at my locker, planning out what I'll say. I'm going to do this. I can talk to Damian, even though he's single. We're friends. We can do this.

I planned out a little script. Just to help me.

He shows up.

"Hi, Damian," I say, looking him right in the eye.

He's nervous and red-faced. "Hi," he says, eyes a

little wide. I think he's surprised I spoke.

You can do this, Maggie! Normal voice. Normal conversation. Do it!

We head down the hallway and I start my lines. “So, did you hear we're gonna have Austin play with us?”

His voice is a little stiff, but he says, “Oh. Yeah, I think I heard something about that.”

“Yeah,” I say, trying to sound fun and lively and confident. “Just three songs, but it'll be fun!”

He's silent. I force myself on.

“Yep. Him and DeAndre and Bill. They're gonna come up and do some pop tunes with us.”

“Oh, yeah,” he says awkwardly. “Man... that'll be fun.”

I'm blowing this. I'm totally blowing this. Damian's not interested at all.

“Yep...” I say, desperate. “Should be fun...”

And then we're at my classroom and I'm devastated because I'd planned this great script and none of it worked and...

Oh, fuck it.

I just turn and walk into my classroom.

Life sucks.

Wednesday.

Well, none of that nonsense yesterday worked, so today I'm not doing a thing. If Damian wants to talk, great. Otherwise, who cares? I'm done trying.

"Hey, good lookin'," he says when he comes up. He's smiling. I can't tell if he's forcing it or not. Is he blushing? I can't tell.

"Hi, Damian," I say, not trying at all.

We start walking down the hall.

"So, um, that's pretty cool about you playing with Austin and them."

"Yeah," I say. "Should be fun."

"You gonna do some Justin Bieber?"

I laugh. "Of course. He's the king. We gotta play the king."

"It'll be a big change from the rest of your songs."

"Well, we're gonna punk them up a little," I say. "And anyway, maybe it'll be like a break in the middle. Or do you think we should mix them in?"

"What do you mean?"

"Well, we have two choices: do all of their songs in one chunk, or mix them in. One of ours, one of theirs, one of ours."

"Oh." He thinks about this and says, "Mix them."

"Yeah, that's what I was thinking, too."

And then we're at my classroom and I realize that Damian and I just had a normal conversation. It wasn't awkward or exhausting. It was just a normal, everyday conversation.

Woo-hoo! Victory!

Thursday.

Okay, this is getting ridiculous. It's Thursday. Damian's been single for how long now? And I haven't even mentioned it?

I need to. Today. I need to show him that I'm all cool with it. It'll make me look... mature? Actually, I have no idea what it will do, but I'm bringing it up anyway. I have to. No more band talk. Today we get serious.

Except that when he gets there, I freak out and get too nervous and we make it all the way down the hall without my saying a word.

I suck.

Thursday night.

We're practicing in Emily's garage. We're going

through a Beyonce song with Austin, DeAndre, and Bill.

Damian's there. He just came to watch. It's made me a wreck the whole night.

We go through Beyonce a few times, punking it up a little, and it's sounding pretty good, so we take a short break. Some people are in the kitchen, some are in the garage. I step out into the driveway to get some fresh air.

Damian's outside.

"Oh, hey," I say, surprised. I briefly consider turning around and racing back inside.

"Hey," he says, smiling.

The sun's not totally down yet, but it's on its way, giving the sky some pretty colors. We're silent. I'm looking at the pink and orange clouds, trying to appear calm. Inside, I'm a mess.

"You and Skyler broke up." I didn't even realize I was going to say it. It just popped out.

Damian's looking up at the sky but I can tell he's not really seeing it. His entire body is tense. "Yep."

Silence.

"So what happened?" I say. "You guys have a fight?"

Damian's silent for a little bit, then he says, "No. I

just... It was time to end it."

"Yeah?"

"Yeah," he says, finally looking at me. "My heart wasn't in it."

We're looking right at each other now, possibly for the first time all week. I'm about to ask him more when Aaron's head pops out and he says, "Hey, guys! Ready to start up again?"

Damn.

Friday.

All during science, I was talking to myself, giving myself a pep talk, building up my courage. Now, standing at my locker, I am 100% going to do it. We *will* have this conversation.

"Hey, good lookin'."

"Hi, Damian."

We start walking.

1, 2, 3, here we go.

"Yesterday, you said your heart wasn't in it? What did you mean by that?"

I did it! Yay me!

Damian's silent. We walk. Finally, he says, "My

heart wasn't in it for a long time. I should have broken up with her a long time ago." He pauses, takes a breath, and says, "There's another girl I've got a crush on. I've had a crush on her a really long time. I just... I didn't really know what to do." He swallows, then adds, "I still don't."

And then we're at my classroom and he says goodbye and races off.

Saturday afternoon.

Band practice. Emily's garage. Austin, DeAndre, and Bill are there with us.

Damian's there, too. Just watching. Just distracting me.

There's another girl I've got a crush on. I'm sure he meant me. Sure of it. Who else could it be? Dammit, it could be anybody! It's not me. It's someone else. But who?

We spend the entire practice eyeing each other from across the room but we never talk. Not one single word.

Who does he have a crush on? It's got to be me, right? God, I hate this.

Sunday.

I spend the entire day in my room, hating myself and my cowardice. I try to call him. I fail.

Monday.

He walks me down the hall. I finally have the courage. I'm going to ask him out. I am 100% ready to do this.

But then Aaron shows up and starts asking me about some crap for the party and he won't shut up and he follows us the whole way down the hall and then it's too late.

Opportunity lost.

Tuesday.

You may not believe it, but I've hardly thought about Damian all day. It's this damn party. It's just days away and we still have a ton of stuff we need to do for it. Standing at my locker, grabbing books, I'm thinking about how I'm going to get all my gear to the party, since I'm also supposed to pick up food. Somebody else is going to have to get the ice. I just won't have time.

When Damian shows up, it actually catches me off-guard a little.

“Hey, good lookin',” he says.

"Oh, hey sweetie," I say, my head full of party stuff.

"What's up?" he asks as we start down the crowded, noisy hallway.

"Oh, it's this party business. Throwing a party is complicated."

"That's why I don't throw them. I just go to them."

"So you're like a professional party-goer now?" I give him a goofy smile.

"I wouldn't say I'm professional," he says. "Nobody's *paying* me to go to their parties. Though they should."

"You're that cool?"

He throws an arm around my shoulder. "Baby doll, I'm the *coolest*. Ain't nobody cool like me." Sadly, he removes his arm.

"Well, sorry, cool guy, but we're not paying you."

"That's a mistake. I might not show up. And then how would you feel?"

I bump him with my shoulder as we walk. "Devastated. We'd probably just send everyone home."

He bumps me back. "Exactly. And you don't want that. You need me there."

"How much do you charge?"

"One burger," he says.

"That's it? A burger? And we get you for the whole entire party?"

"A bargain at any price."

"What if we give you a burger *and* a drink?"

"I take off my shirt."

I pretend to swoon and grab hold of his arm, breathless. "And a burger, a drink, and some chips?"

"Oh, you don't want that..." he says, shaking his head. "Things get a little out of control then. You should just stop with the burger and the drink. We don't want the cops showing up."

We've reached my classroom, but I'm still holding his shoulder, acting like an adoring fan. "But maybe I *do* want that," I say, my voice low.

"You want the cops showing up?"

"No, I just want to find out what you do that *makes* the cops show up."

We're standing there and I'm hanging all over him and he's giving me this silly rock star look and our faces are totally close. "Well, in that case," he says, so quietly that only I can hear, "go ahead and give me the chips. It could be fun."

We stay like that a few seconds more, super-close, our noses almost touching. Then we break apart. He heads down the hall and I go into my class.

I sit in my usual spot, right next to Audrey, and I can barely breathe. Dear God, that was the *best*. That was the best it's been since he left Skyler.

All this horrible crap from the last week and a half? All this nervousness and awkwardness? I'm going to put all of that behind me. From now on, I'm not going to *try* to get Damian. I'm just going to *be*. Sort of like I was just now. I'm gonna be me, he's gonna be him, and if it happens, it happens. But I'm not going to be a nervous wreck anymore. I refuse. I'm just going to get the band ready, get the party ready, and be at peace regarding Damian Shaw.

Chapter 30

So it's the next day. Wednesday. Sunny. Warm. Perfect, really. School's done, but I'm still here, sitting on a bench in the courtyard, waiting for my dad to finish with a parent-teacher conference.

Yeah, I know, right? My dad, here at school, talking to my English teacher. I'm not sweating it or anything – my grades are fine – but it's still weird having him here, seeing him walking the halls. So out of place. So old. And so *tall*. I forget how tall my dad is, but seeing him standing next to lockers or sitting in a classroom, it really stands out.

But that's not really what I'm thinking about, sitting there in the sun. I'm thinking about everything that's happened to me in the last year. Because today's the one-year anniversary of my mom's death.

One year ago today, I woke up, got dressed, and had breakfast with her. We had a tiny argument about whether I could go to Becky's house that night, then she gave me a kiss on the cheek and went out to her car. A few minutes later, I walked to the bus stop and went to school. Went through my day, sat through my classes, talked with my friends, never realizing it was the last normal day of my life. If I'd known Mom was going to die on her drive home that night, if I'd known that everything was going to change, maybe I would have done the day differently. Paid more attention, at least.

But no, it was a normal day. Just like today.

So I'm sitting here, face up to the sun, trying not to think about her too much. And failing.

Way over on the other side of the courtyard, I see my old friends Becky and Ginger and a bunch of other girls, all giggly and gossipy, walking toward the student parking lot. They're wearing all the right clothes, saying all the right things, heading to all the right cars. Becky's very solidly in the popular crowd these days. She'll be invited to Robbie McMorrison's party.

If Mom hadn't been in that car crash, would Becky and I still be friends? Would I be in the popular crowd right now? Would big, dopey Maggie the Sasquatch be walking with those girls? Wearing those clothes? Talking about... whatever it is girls like that talk about?

"Hey, Maggie!"

I look over and there's Aaron Johnson, walking toward me with a couple of his friends. He's carrying his skateboard.

"What up, skater boy?"

"We're going to Sibilia Park. You want in? We might hit Youngblood's after."

"Tempting, but I'm waiting on my dad. He's having a conference with Mr. Regnier."

"You in trouble?" one of his friends asks.

"No. I'm not sure why they're meeting. Maybe just to meet. I don't know. But anyway, you guys go ahead."

"Come on," Aaron says. "It'll be fun."

"So would Arleta's with Audrey, but I turned her down, didn't I?"

"Your boyfriend will be disappointed," Aaron says, giving me an evil grin.

I refuse to rise to the bait.

"Who's her boyfriend?" one of his friends asks.

"Damian Shaw."

"He's not my boyfriend," I say in a relaxed, happy voice, refusing to let them annoy me.

"Not yet," Aaron says. "But, seriously, a bunch of them are playing ball on the courts there. You should come."

I tell them no, but thank you, then we talk about nothing for a few minutes and they head off to the student parking lot, slouching along like a bunch of skate punks. Which, of course, is exactly the look they're going for.

So there you are. Where would I be if Mom hadn't died? Those are my two choices.

Becky and Ginger. The popular crowd. Robbie McMorrison's parties.

Or vintage clothes with Audrey. Friends with a bunch of jazz band skate punks. Crushing on a basketball player.

I sit there in the courtyard, enjoying the spring weather and thinking about this. It's not a perfect comparison – not a black and white choice – because even if Mom were alive, I might still have gone to David Nelson's auditions, right? I might still have drifted away from Becky. I might still have become friends with Audrey. Damian and I might still be... whatever the hell Damian and I are. What are we, anyway? I have no friggin' idea. But we might still be it, even if Mom were alive. I wonder if she'd like him? But that's crazy. Of course she'd like him. She'd love him.

And for some reason, that's the thought that finally makes my eyes fill with tears. All day, I've been just fine, but now, thinking about Mom meeting Damian, that's what makes me well up.

"Hey, good lookin'."

Oh, dear Jesus. Perfect timing.

"Dammit, Damian," I say, wiping my eyes. "Why do you have to catch me when I'm crying? I was fine just two minutes ago. You couldn't have walked up then?"

"Why are you crying?" he says, sitting next to me on the bench.

"I'm not, really," I say, sniffing and trying to smile at him. "It was nothing. Just thinking about stuff." I blink a few times. "My mom."

He starts rubbing my back, looking all sweet and sympathetic and perfect. All thoughts of Mom are completely gone. We're silent for a bit, which is nice, but then I ask him why he's not down at the park with his boys.

"Oh, well..." He gets a little red-faced then and clears his throat. "I just wanted to, erm... I wanted to ask you if you... I don't know what you're doing tomorrow... probably something with Audrey... getting ready for the party, probably... erm... and that's fine, but... you know, if you're not... I thought maybe you might want to... I mean, you and me... I mean, you and I... we could..."

At first I don't know what he's going on about or why he's so nervous, but then my heart stops and I realize, oh, dear God... this is it, isn't it? He's asking me out!

Well, no surprise, this sends me into a full-on panic, and my face bursts into flames and I sort of want to get up and run away in terror, but I don't, I stay there, frozen in fear, and he's still stuttering and trying to talk and it's both wonderful and horrible and I'm completely terrified and completely excited, and then –

"Well, hey, you two!"

It's my dad.

Worst. Timing. Ever.

Damian shoots to his feet. "Oh, hi! Hi, Mr. Blackman!" He's shaking Dad's hand, his face bright red.

"So, what are you two up to?"

"Oh, nothing," Damian says, totally nervous. "Just hanging out. Just talking. Nothing, really."

Dad's clueless, of course, and asks Damian if he saw some stupid basketball game and so they start talking about that. I sit there on my bench, furious. Silently murdering my father, over and over.

I don't know how long they talk, the friggin' idiots, but it's long enough that I calm down and stop killing them both in my head. Instead, I start watching Dad and how he's smiling and laughing with Damian. How happy he is, just talking about sports.

And for some reason, that's what makes me realize that it's not just my mom who died one year ago today. His wife died, too.

I can't believe how clueless I've been. How thoughtless. As tough as this day's been for me, it's probably been worse for him. I'm sure he's been thinking about the past year, just like I have. Thinking about who he used to be. Who he is now. Wondering how life would be different if Mom were still alive.

All the drinking he's done in the last year? All those nights he's cried, all those nights downstairs listening to sad songs, watching old movies? All of that's because of what happened one year ago today. When his wife left work and never made it home.

And this should probably be embarrassing, but I'm just overcome by the thought of it, so I stand up from my bench and wrap Dad up in a big hug. It totally interrupts his sports talk with Damian, which they have a little laugh about, and Dad says, "Well, I guess I better get this one home." We tell Damian goodbye, then Dad and I walk out to his car in front of the school and start heading home.

It's been a tough year for me and Dad. A tough, tough year. But maybe we've made it through the worst. Maybe surviving this first year is the hardest part and it'll all be smooth from here. I mean, look at us. Dad's hardly drinking at all anymore, and I pretty much never burst into tears. Dad's got this new job offer, and I've got a rock band and a bunch of new friends. Dad can still have his silly, happy conversations about sports, and I've got a cute boy who wants to ask me out.

Yep. Maybe we've made it, me and Dad. Maybe it's all easy from here on.

Except it doesn't last. Dad seems a little quiet when we stop at the store on the way home. And I can see his face sinking lower as we make dinner. And he has a scotch while we eat. And then another. It's almost like I can see him disappearing. And I have no idea how to stop it.

So when he goes into the den and turns on the TV, I know it's not to watch sports. And when he starts playing Mom's favorite movie, I know that the worst's not over. That we're still not healed. That it will take more than one year for this family to be okay again.

And that's what I think about as I lie in my darkened bedroom, trying to fall asleep while Mom's favorite songs are blasting downstairs. I'm not sure what time it is when I finally drift off, but Dad's still down there, getting drunk and mourning his wife deep into the night.

Chapter 31

I don't know quite how, but somehow I forget to set my alarm clock, so the next morning I wake up late. I mean, seriously late. I not only miss the bus, I'm already late for first period. Dammit.

As I throw on some clothes, I wonder what the hell I'm going to do. Looking out the window, I can see that Dad's already left for work, so he can't give me a lift. I can't call Audrey, she's in class. Wait... Damian doesn't have a first period class! I grab my phone and call him.

He's in the school parking lot when I reach him, but says he'll turn around and come pick me up. "But you owe me," he says.

What I owe him, I have no idea, nor do I really care. All I know is that Damian's single, he almost asked me out yesterday, and now he's going to drive me to school just like we're boyfriend and girlfriend. I've got a smile on my face as I throw on some clothes, shove food into my mouth, and race out to meet him in the driveway. He's laughing at me as I slide into the passenger seat.

"Shut up, Damian."

"You've still got pillow marks on your face."

"Don't make fun of me. Do I really? Well, whatever. Let's just go. I'm late enough as it is. Do I really have pillow face? Thanks for coming to get me, by the way."

"Glad to. And yes, you do. You look different. No makeup?"

"No."

"I like it. You should look like this every day. It's adorable."

"Shut up."

I'm not even the tiniest bit mad, of course. He raced across town to pick me up, just like a boyfriend would. And he called me adorable.

He starts backing out of our driveway when a cop car pulls to a stop right there in front of my house.

"Whoa," Damian says, coming to a halt. "Did I do something wrong? Am I not allowed to back up here?"

I don't know what to tell him. I have basically zero

experience with cops. Have *I* done something wrong? This is because I'm late for school, isn't it?

The cop opens his door and steps out of his car. God, I'm screwed.

"What do we do?" Damian says in a half-whisper.

The cop's walking over to us and we're silent and tense. When he gets to the car, he knocks lightly on Damian's window. We both jump a little and Damian rolls down his window.

"Um, hi," Damian says. "Am I not allowed to back out of here?"

"You live here, son?"

Damian shakes his head and point a thumb at me. "She does."

The cops leans down and looks over at me. "You live here?"

What did I do? I must have done something. "Yes, sir."

"With Stephen Blackman?"

"Yes, sir."

"You're his daughter?"

"Yes, sir."

"Anybody else here? Your mother, maybe?"

"No. Um, my mother... she died."

"Oh," he says. "I'm sorry. So it's just you and your dad?"

"Yes, sir."

"No one else?"

I shake my head no. I'm totally confused. What the hell's going on here?

The cop is quiet for a few seconds, looking like he's not sure what do. Finally, he says, "Well, I'm sorry to tell you this, but your dad was out last night, driving under the influence. Wrecked his car. He's at the hospital right now."

I'm not really sure what happens after that.

Chapter 32

I have no memory of Damian driving me to the hospital, but somehow we're here. We're standing at the front desk and I'm in a complete fog and Damian is asking the lady how we can find Stephen Blackman and then we're on an elevator and we're walking down hallways and we come to another desk and he's talking to another lady, then we're walking into a room and there are curtains everywhere and beeping machines and four beds. The beds have people in them, people I don't know, but then behind the last curtain, in the last bed, is my dad.

He's alive.

He looks awful, but he's alive.

I rush up to him, but when I get there I don't know

what to do. I want to hug him, but he's got wires and tubes and IV drips and there's this rolling table thing across his bed with a tray of food on it.

He looks *horrible*. His entire face is beaten up and swollen, like he's been in a huge fight. Part of his head's been shaved and there's a long line of stitches going from the top of his head down to his forehead. There are stitches below his nose, too, and his lips are swollen and discolored.

His eyes were half-closed before, but now he opens them and looks at me. They're watery and unfocused.

In a whisper, I say, "Oh, Dad..."

One of his arms is in a cast, but he starts moving the other one toward me. I can see how hard it is for him, so I just reach out and grab it. Tears are pouring down my cheeks.

"Are you okay, Dad? What happened?"

Dad blinks and his eyes are shiny and he tries to say something but his lips are just too swollen, so it comes out a whispered mumble.

"It's okay, Dad. You don't have to talk. I'm here and I love you."

Tears start running down his cheeks, too, and I worry for a moment that it will mess up the stitches around his mouth, so I reach out and try to stop the tears with my finger but then I'm worried I'll hurt his face, it's so messed up, so I just hold his hand and cry. I don't know how long the two of us are like that. Five minutes? Ten? An hour? It feels like forever.

Eventually, there's a doctor there and she's talking to me. I'm still holding Dad's hand, but his eyes are closed now, so I look at the doctor and she talks and I nod my head, but I swear to God, I don't hear a thing she says. Not a single thing.

Finally, she takes off and I sit there holding Dad's hand, right next to his bed. Time passes, I don't know how long. Dad's sleeping, I'm thinking. Thinking about Mom dying and what I would do if Dad died, too. I think about God and why He hates me so much. Just when my life was turning around, God decides to hit me with this.

For whatever reason, I suddenly need to move, so I stand up and put Dad's hand back on his bed, then I walk out of the big room with its beds and its curtains and its goddamn beeping machines. I'm walking down the hall, walking really fast, and there are rooms everywhere and every single one has beds and machines and people in pain and I just want to scream and hit something. And then I'm out of the hallways and into this open area near the elevators and there's this big window with this big view and I can see forever and I lean against it and start crying. And then Damian's there and he's holding me and I'm crying against his chest and he's saying stuff like it's okay, it's okay, it'll be alright, but I'm not sure I agree with him. I mean, God hates me. How is that going to be alright? You can't escape God hating you.

But he holds me and rubs my back and says soft things and eventually my crying slows down and then we're sitting on a bench there and I'm staring out the big windows, out over the trees and the houses, off to the horizon. Damian's sitting there with me, holding my hand, and I slowly calm down.

Eventually, I say, “I didn't hear a thing the doctor said. Did you?”

“Yeah.”

“Was it bad?”

“No, actually. She said your dad's not as bad as he looks. The stitches are no big deal, there's no cracked skull or anything. The arm's broken, but it's not the worst break in the world. And it's in the cast, obviously. He's on some pain meds, so he's a little out of it, but it's nothing serious. She said he could come home tonight, believe it or not.”

I don't say anything while Damian tells me all this. I just sit there, holding his hand in both of mine, still looking out the big windows, still seeing nothing.

“I called school and told them what happened,” he says.

I nod.

"I called Audrey, too. Left a voicemail."

I nod again.

"I can talk to the nurses if you want and ask them how we're supposed to get your dad home. It might be an ambulance or something. I don't know. If it's not, we can take him in my car."

I give a silent laugh and say, "I guess we don't have a car anymore."

After a pause, he says, "No, I guess not."

For the first time, I look at him. He's looking at me like he's worried I'll break. I can't say I blame him. I look down at my lap, where I have his hand clasped between both of mine. I turn his hand over and interlace our fingers. I wonder briefly if he wants his hand back, then decide I don't care. I pull it up to my chest and rest it on my heart, then scoot over so our sides touch and my head rests on his shoulder. He leans his head over so it rests on the top of mine.

This is the most intimate we've ever been. And it's in a hospital. With my dad all banged up down the hall. I have no idea how to feel about this. I just know that I feel so much love for Damian right now. So much.

I don't know how long we sit there, but eventually we make our way back to Dad's room. I'm in better shape now. I can actually have a conversation with the nurse, then later, the doctor. They pretty much confirm everything Damian said. Dad looks bad, and he's a little loopy with pain meds, but for the most part he's fine. We can discharge him whenever we're ready. An ambulance will take him home.

And so that's what we do. I sign Dad out. It's a little weird with the paperwork, since I'm not 18, but there's no one else to sign. There are no adults. Anywhere. Just me and Dad.

Damian takes me home. I hold his hand while we drive.

When we get to the house, Audrey's waiting there in the driveway. She races up and gives me a giant hug and looks like she's about to burst into tears, but I tell her I'm okay, which I guess I basically am now. So then we're all inside, sitting around, waiting for the ambulance to show up, and it's a little weird, since it's the first time all day I haven't been in the friggin' hospital. It just feels weird to be back in the real world, you know?

Plus, Damian had been so perfect at the hospital. He'd held me and comforted me and... I don't know... been my *boyfriend*, more or less. And a perfect boyfriend, at that. So what happens now? Is all that love gone? Do we just go back to the way it used to be?

So that's what I'm thinking about as the three of us sit around the kitchen table. Audrey's asking lots of questions and I'm answering some and Damian's answering others. I'm holding Dad's wallet, which I found on the kitchen counter. He must have gone out last night without it. What the hell was he thinking, going out drunk?

Eventually, the doorbell rings and it's the ambulance guys and they're carrying this bed-thing with Dad strapped to it, so things get a little crazy. We're moving furniture out of their way and I'm trying to figure out where to put Dad. He's awake now, so he's saying to put him on the sofa, though he's still a little mumbley and hard to understand with his swollen, stitched-up mouth. He's on those pain meds, too, so who knows if he's thinking clearly, but whatever, fine, just put him on the couch.

And then the ambulance guys are gone and Dad looks awful but I don't really know what to do, so I just get him comfortable with a blanket and a pillow and he says to just let him sleep, so that's what I do.

Audrey and Damian are sitting around the kitchen table again. I want to sit next to Damian, but I'm not sure I'm allowed to. I could have at the hospital.

So I sit next to Audrey and she puts her hand on mine and tells me it'll all be okay. Damian told me that earlier and I didn't really believe him, but I guess I'm feeling a little less hopeless now. I mean, Dad's home and he's not dying and I've got friends here and Damian's been super-sweet all day, so I guess things can't be too bad.

Outside, the sun's starting to go down and I realize that I haven't eaten anything since that morning. It seems like a lifetime ago. So I root around in the kitchen for a little bit and Audrey and Damian help and before long we've got some spaghetti going. I'm not really sure what to do about food for Dad. Actually, I'm not sure about *anything* regarding Dad. I'm not a nurse.

I go into the living room and wake him up and he's a little out of it and a little mumbley, but eventually says he'd like some spaghetti. First though, he needs to use the restroom, so I try helping him get up but can't quite do it and then Damian swoops in – I swear to God, I would marry Damian right now if he asked – and between the two of us, we get Dad up. He tells me to run into the den and get my granddad's old cane that's in the closet, so I get that and then, believe it or not, Dad can kind of hobble his way into the bathroom and take care of things himself. Thank God, right? What if I'd had to help him in there? I'm not sure I could. But I guess the doctor was right. He looks worse than he actually is. Lots of bruises, lots of stitches, a broken arm, but mostly he's okay.

Standing there in the hallway, waiting for Dad to come out, I lean against Damian. He puts his arms around me and I rest my face against his neck, breathing him in, and it's like we're back at the hospital.

I wish I could stay like this forever.

But we break it up when Dad comes out. We move to help him, but he waves us off and, slowly, deliberately, painfully, makes his way down the hall, past the couch, and all the way to the kitchen table, where, with a little help, he sits down. By the end of it all, he's exhausted, but says he'll have some spaghetti.

Well, that's an ordeal, of course, since his mouth's all swollen and stitched up, but eventually we figure out how to mash it up and get it in. I say “we” figure it out, but in truth, by the end, Dad doesn't want any help. He wants to do as much as he can. What he's capable of doing, I have no idea. Can he get upstairs to his bed tonight? Probably not. Maybe tomorrow. What about taking a bath? Dear God, I don't even want to think about that.

So the four of us eat spaghetti. It's a little tense. We're mostly just watching Dad. He's silent and slow. It's not easy for him to eat, but he does it, somehow. He looks exhausted. It's exhausting just watching him.

Eventually, he puts his fork down, but doesn't make any indication he wants to get up.

“You want to go back to the couch, Dad?”

He shakes his head. After a bit, he says, “I need to talk to you.” He's working really hard to speak clearly. It's not easy.

Audrey and Damian look uncertain and Audrey says, "We can go in the other room if you want."

"No," Dad says. "You should hear this, too. You're Maggie's friends."

He pauses then, like he needs to catch his breath or regain his strength or something. Then he sits up straight and says, "I almost killed myself last night." He's looking at the table as he talks. "I drove drunk and I almost died." He's trying hard to enunciate, but it's tough with his mouth. "I don't know why I got in the car. I don't even remember doing it. But I almost killed myself. And you would've been an orphan."

He looks up at me then and his eyes are wet and I can tell he's close to crying and my dad *never* cries, so of course, tears start pouring down my face and Audrey's holding my hand, but I let Dad keep talking.

"I've been a bad father, Maggie," he says through swollen lips. "But that's over. I'm done drinking. Completely. Not even a beer. Ever." He pauses and sniffs and uses a napkin to wipe his eyes and I'm just a wreck, but I let him go on. "I'm going to start going to AA meetings. Starting tomorrow. I'd go right now, but I don't think my body could take it. Tomorrow, though. I don't know how I'll get there. Maybe the bus."

"I'll take you," Damian says, quickly and firmly.

Dad looks at him and nods. "Thanks." He's quiet for a bit, then says, "So that's that. No more drinking.

And I'm sorry. You deserve better. I hope you can forgive me."

And then he's done. And I can tell he's done. So I put my arms around him as best I can without hurting him and I hug him and tell him I love him. Which I do.

And then Dad says he's ready for bed and thinks he can get upstairs. And mostly he can, but Damian walks up beside him and maybe gives him a little help a couple times and then they disappear into Dad's room and Audrey and I are out in the hall and it's quiet.

I feel like a dishrag that's been wrung out dry. I'm as tired as I've ever been. My life has changed completely today, but I'm too tired to fully grasp all of it. Do I have a boyfriend now? What about the party on Saturday? Is it still on? Is my band still playing it?

And the biggest question of all: do I have my dad back? I sort of think I do. These next few days are going to be tough, but I'm pretty sure my dad's back. Really back. And that probably matters more than all the rest of it put together.

Chapter 33

"Dad! Lunch is ready!" I'm yelling up the stairs. "Are you?"

He appears at the top of the stairs, fully dressed, Granddad's cane by his side, and starts slowly making his way down.

"Are you sure you're okay?" I say, walking tentatively a few stairs towards him.

"Yes," he says, grunting with effort. "Just gimme a second. I'm moving slow. You don't have to watch. I've got this."

It's hard to walk away, but I retreat to the kitchen anyway. It's only been two days since the accident, but Dad's pushing hard to get back up and running.

Nothing is easy for him, but he wants to do it, so I let him.

It's Saturday, by the way. Day of the party. Dad absolutely refused to let me cancel it. Audrey is coming to get me soon, but for now, it's lunch.

Dad's mouth is a lot better, but he's still not real happy chewing, so I've made us some tuna fish salad. I've got mine in a sandwich, Dad's is just in a bowl. I should have made it into a salad or something. With tomatoes and lettuce. Maybe next time.

"Finally!" Dad says when he enters the kitchen, his forehead shiny with sweat. His arm's still in a cast and he's still got the stitches on the forehead and the upper lip. His face is less swollen, but the bruises are darker and uglier. His biggest complaint, though, is just being sore all over. He didn't hurt his legs, thank goodness, but he still limps along with the cane, every step painful, his traumatized body complaining. "Thanks, baby," he says, sitting at the table and picking up his fork.

It's a gorgeous day. Warm, sunny. The perfect day for a pool party.

"Your boyfriend coming to pick you up?" Dad says, giving me a mischievous look.

"He's not my boyfriend," I say, not the least bit upset.

"Not yet, at least."

I'm unable to hold back a small smile. "Not yet."

At this point, it's no longer a question of "if." Just a question of "when." These last few days have made it clear. Damian's just as crazy for me as I am for him.

I realize I'm grinning like an idiot now, so I shove my sandwich into my mouth before Dad starts teasing me.

Yeah, it's only a matter of time. Maybe today. Maybe tomorrow. Maybe next week.

Hopefully today.

While we eat, Dad tells me he's got an angle on another car for us. A little Japanese two-door. Some guy in one of his AA meetings told him he'd sell it cheap. Dad's going to multiple meetings every day. I suppose that'll slow down once he heads back to work on Monday, but he'll still go at least once a day.

I think so, at least.

I hope so.

I have no idea. We're in uncharted territory here. I'll just hope for the best.

We're finishing up lunch when the doorbell rings. It's Reggie, Dad's "sponsor." That's what they call the guy in AA who you can call if you're ever having a hard time staying sober. I think that's what sponsors do, at least. And maybe they give you rides to meetings, too. This one does.

While Dad's making his slow way out to Reggie's car, Audrey pulls up in front of the house, so I grab my bass and my amp and start lugging them out there. My arms don't look any more muscular than they used to, but I can't imagine why, as much as I haul this heavy-ass stuff around.

“You look cute,” Audrey says as I load it all into her car. “I like that dress. You got your swimsuit?”

“I do. You?”

“It's at the house. Austin's gonna frickin' love it.”

“I wish I knew what Damian liked. I'm really nervous.”

“He'll like it. You could wear a scuba diver's wetsuit and he'd like it.”

“I'm still nervous. We'll be *swimming* together.”

“More than swimming, I hope.”

When we get to Audrey's, we start carrying stuff from her house to the clubhouse. Food, drinks, coolers, bags of ice. Aaron shows up to help with the last few things, then pulls his drum kit out of his car and starts setting it up. There's a big giant deck, but we're going to play inside so we don't disturb the neighbors. While Aaron's setting up his kit, some little kids wander up from the pool in their wet swimsuits, watching us through the sliding glass doors, wondering what's going on. They're probably nine or ten.

"We're having a concert later!" Audrey yells at them. "You should come back and watch!" They squeal and race back to the pool. "They're probably asking their moms right now if they can come."

Emily shows up then and brings in her guitar stuff. She's all excited because Audrey's going to dye her hair for the concert.

"You're sure about this?" I ask.

"Totally," she says, beaming. "And it's just temporary, anyway. It's just temporary, right, Audrey?"

"In a week, no one will have any idea that you were once a purple-haired rock star."

"Let's do it!"

So we leave Aaron to guard the clubhouse, head back to Audrey's, and all crowd into her bathroom. It's sort of fun watching Audrey play beautician, and Emily's all giggly and silly, so that's fun, but in the end, it's just too crowded, so I decide to head back to the clubhouse.

"Hey, sweetie," Audrey's mom Ingrid says to me in the entryway. "Come in here and grab this stuff for the party. You forgot a bag."

"Oh, sorry. Thanks."

"Are you excited?" She looks like she wishes she was still a teenager herself.

"Yeah. A little nervous."

"You know, Maggie, I'm so glad you and Audrey became friends. You've been so good for her."

"I have?"

"Oh, absolutely," she says. "She's so much happier since she met you. Rebecca and I were talking about it just the other day. She's just happier and sunnier and more positive. She's like a different girl."

I'm kind of amazed by this. It seems so backwards. I feel like Audrey's the one who's helped *me*, not the other way around. I don't think I can say this to Ingrid, though, so I just say thanks, grab the bag, and head over to the clubhouse, my head swimming.

Well, Aaron and I get everything in the clubhouse squared away and eventually people start showing up. I'm nervous, trying to be a good host, showing them where the food is, where the drinks are. I wish Audrey and Emily would get back. Aaron's pretty worthless for this.

"Hey, good lookin'."

I turn and it's Damian and I'm so glad to see him, I just fall into his arms for a big hug. It's totally pathetic, but I don't care. “Finally!” I say. “You can help me with all these people. I don't know what to do with them all.”

“They look okay to me,” he says. “What's your worry?”

“I don't know,” I say. He's still holding me, by the way. It's awesome. “I don't really know how parties work.”

Austin's next to us then. “Where are we playing, boss?”

I reluctantly leave Damian's arms to show Austin where I want him to set up and we run electrical cords for amps. Typical band stuff.

People are continuing to show up and I can see Damian over there welcoming them. He's the best. It's a little past four, still hot and sunny, so a lot people are just putting on their swimsuits – the clubhouse has boys and girls bathrooms – and heading down to the pool. I can see the first few people down there already, goofing around. It's super easy for someone to race back up here to get some food or use the bathroom or something.

People continue to arrive. I'm kind of amazed a bunch of dorks like us could fill a clubhouse, but it looks like we might actually do it.

A bunch of Aaron's jazz band friends have showed

up. One of them even has a girlfriend.

DeAndre shows up, plus a couple guys from the basketball team. They immediately want food, but DeAndre's playing with us later, so I make him set up his kick drum and tambourine and stuff.

“I want you here,” I tell him. “Next to Emily.”

“When do we go on?”

“When it starts getting dark. A couple hours, maybe.”

“And we're starting with the Elvis song?”

I want to pull my hair out. “DeAndre! How many times... We're not doing the Elvis song! Beyonce, Bieber, Madonna. That's it.”

“Fine, fine. Sorry I asked.”

Running a band is a pain in the ass. Don't let anyone tell you differently.

“Let's go swimming,” Damian says, throwing an arm around my shoulders. He's been so touchy and affectionate this week. It's fabulous. I wish he'd kiss me, already. I should kiss *him*. Like, right now. Just do it. Right here in front of God and everyone. Nobody would care, would they?

But of course I don't.

“Hold on,” I tell him. “People are still showing up.”

Emily's little sister shows up with some of her freshmen friends. They look young, but Aaron doesn't seem to mind. He and some of his friends are over there flirting. Pathetic.

Right after them, who walks in but David Nelson and John Knowlson, fresh off their triumphant performance last night at the North Sycamore Follies.

The Follies were so fun. We all went. Sat in the front row of the balcony. Tons and tons of acts, but David and his band went on last. They were great, of course, but, I dunno, it was maybe a little slow for me. Real impressive performance, but like I've said, not all that fun. I'm not having any regrets.

Finally, *finally*, Audrey and Emily show up and Emily's got dark purple hair. It looks totally fabulous and everyone's oo-ing and ah-ing over it and she's loving all the attention and then her boyfriend Simon shows up and he doesn't know *what* to think – I don't think she told him she was going to do it – but whatever, everyone else likes it.

"Let's go swimming," Damian says to me again. "The party's going fine. Let's go."

I'm suddenly terrified and I sort of crumple up against his chest and say, "I'm scared."

Well, he just starts belly-laughing at this, so I punch him in the chest and he pulls me closer and says, "I want to see you in a bikini."

I'm smiling and blushing. "Stop it."

"Is it hot? I bet it's hot."

"*Stop* it," I say, hiding my smile in his chest. "I'm scared."

"Go change," he says, letting go of me. "That's an order, Blackman. I'll change, too."

So we go change in the bathrooms and I come out with a towel wrapped around me, so he's all disappointed about that, but whatever, I'm nervous, so we get down to the pool and he jumps in and is just treading water there, looking up at me, being a *complete* dick, and I'm laughing and blushing and I tell him to turn around but he won't, so I throw off my towel and jump in as fast as I can and he's laughing and then he swims over and kisses me.

Yes! He kisses me! Right there in the pool!

It's not a big kiss. There's no tongue. It's more a peck than anything, but who cares, right? So I'm like totally shocked and excited, and I chase after him but he's swimming away and I swear, I want to kill him, but he's just too fast, so I never get to grab him and kiss him back, the jerk.

So, the swimming pool's really pretty big, and there's tons of people there from the neighborhood – parents and kids and what all – but there's also a lot of kids from our party, so a few people start chicken-fighting and they challenge me and Damian to a fight. Well, it's not even fair. I mean, I'm six feet tall and Damian's six-three, so when I'm sitting on his shoulders like that, it's truly no contest. We absolutely dominate everybody until a couple of guys from the basketball team pair up, and that's not really fair because they're both guys, but whatever, it's fun.

So after we've been beaten, we sort of swim around a little, not doing anything special. I want to kiss him again but I don't. There's people around. And I'm a coward.

Eventually we decide to head up to the clubhouse, get some food, and get ready for the show. Getting out of the pool, I'm aware that he can totally see me in my bikini, but whatever. I was sitting on his shoulders earlier. I don't think you can be bashful after that.

Up at the clubhouse, Austin's got the grill fired up, so we get some burgers and eat them there on the deck. I've got my towel wrapped around me, but Damian's just sitting there in his swim trunks, all cute and wet. When we finish the burgers, we go inside and change back into our clothes, although it's new clothes for me this time. Audrey and I spent a lot of time figuring out what I should wear for the show. It's all vintage, of course. Blue. Tight-fitting. A tiny little pillbox hat. Audrey calls it the “1960s Transatlantic Stewardess” look. She's so dramatic.

When I finally come out, I head into the main room,

milling around, looking for Damian.

"Dude!" Aaron says when he sees me. "You look awesome!"

"You ready to play?" I ask him. "Go get changed."

"When do we go on?"

I look at my phone, up at the sky, down towards the slowly-emptying pool. "Half an hour."

I move around the party some more. Things are going surprisingly well. Everyone seems happy. Maybe throwing a party's not as hard as I'd thought.

"You look fabulous!" Emily says when she sees me.

"You do, too," I say. "*Love* the hair. You ready to play? Half an hour?"

She looks a little terrified, but says she's ready. She's dressed cool, too. Audrey's work, of course.

I still can't find Damian, so I head out to the deck. Austin's still manning the grill, cooking burgers and dogs.

"Oh, you look hot!" he says. "Has Damian seen that?"

"I can't find him."

Austin uses his barbecue tongs to point across the deck and I finally see him, over there with DeAndre, goofing off. As I walk over, they stop their conversation and stare. Damian's mouth hangs open a tiny bit.

I reach out and take his hand. “Follow me.”

We go back through the clubhouse and then out the front door, me leading him along by the hand. I don't think, I just walk. If I think, I'll get scared and stop, so I don't.

Out front it's quiet and still and private. I turn and face him and draw his hands to my waist.

“I'm not sure which I like better,” he says, his voice low in the new-found quiet. “You in this outfit or in the bikini. You're hot both ways.”

I'm scared. If I think, I'll chicken out, so I don't. I just pull Damian towards me and kiss him. A real kiss this time. A deep kiss, a passionate kiss. A kiss that releases everything we've been holding in for all these months.

Remember how much I liked kissing Diego? Well, double that. Triple it. We kiss and we kiss and then we kiss some more. It's fabulous.

I don't know how much time passes, but eventually Audrey pokes her head out and says, “Um, Maggie? Sorry. But it's time to go on. The band's ready. Everyone's waiting.”

I take a second to collect myself, gather my wits, straighten my clothes. Finally, I look at Damian and say, "How do I look?"

He smiles and says, "Hot."

"Good enough for me."

I give him a quick peck, then head back inside. I walk through the waiting crowd, over to our makeshift stage. Everything I've gone through in the past year is finally coming together. All the work, all the trouble, all the pain. Failed bands. Lost friends. A drunk father. Falling out of the car on my first date. All of that's behind me. And now I'm here.

I grab my bass, step up to the mike, and nod to the others. Aaron counts us off and we play.

Connect with the author online

I'm all over the place online. Search me out on Twitter, Facebook, and Goodreads.

I've also got a soccer column called "Six Degrees" at sliderulepass.net and a radio show called "Six Degrees of Rockination" at kzme.fm.

And if you're looking to buy another book, you can use Amazon, Smashwords, Apple, Barnes & Noble, Kobo, and assorted others.

Made in the USA
San Bernardino, CA
21 April 2014